Monday April 9

Woke up with a headache. Probably allergies. Took the bus to work and must have hit every red light on the way. Stood for a while and got a seat. A few blocks later, a couple ladies got on. I should have given up my seat, but pretended I didn't see them. My guilt was short-lived. Seats opened up soon enough.

Bob got canned today at work. Not straight out fired, just taken off the schedule indefinitely. "We'll call you when we need you." We all knew it was coming. He never cleaned or dusted his counter. I heard he'd had some customer complaints. People thought he could be snippy. We could not be snippy and keep this job. Rumor was Bob had a drinking problem. He was going through a divorce, but I'm not sure if the drinking was the cause or effect. At least that's what Ella, who works in Payroll, said. She can't keep a secret to save her life. Not that she has ever tried. Loves getting her nose into everybody's business. Some say she's a spy for management, but I think she's just nosy. Ella said they had Bob's final check waiting, and then she let out that horrible cackle of hers. Nails on a chalkboard. She was always flirting with the guys in Housewares. She said she did not know of any other layoffs coming. I heard they are looking for someone younger to replace Bob.

Reginald was back to his old tricks this afternoon, coming around and asking me where I went for lunch last Sunday, knowing for a fact I went to Midtown for the buffet. When I said the word "buffet," he turned and looked at his buddies at the next station, and I heard them whisper the word "pansy." Something about the way I said it. *Schoolboys.*

You have nowhere to go when you're stuck behind a counter, but you become very good at giving a vacant smile and puttering about. When I heard the laughter, that's what I did. The Housewares guys eventually quieted down and went on to the next prank. They're never chastised. They think they are above everyone because they are in Appliances and attached to big-ticket sales. Every one of them has homes and mortgages and wives and horrible, screeching children who will one day be just as hateful as their fathers. My guess is that the Appliances crew want to make everyone else miserable too.

Sold four ties to one gentleman today. That helps my weekly sales and commission. *Yay!* The floor manager saw me boxing them and smiled. *Double yay!* That was a relief after the Bob incident. You always have to be on your toes here. If someone isn't producing, the management is fond of replacing them with people who will, or drastically cutting a fellow's hours. The divide between us and them is very large at M_____. And I am not even much a part of the 'us'.

After work, I had dinner at Mason's and saw *The Music Man* at the State Theater. No mischief was going on in the theater. The movie was enjoyable, but not much more than that. I prefer the original cast recording from Broadway. I liked Buddy Hackett. When the movie ended, I was happy to discover the weather had warmed a bit. The fresh air felt great. I walked down State, across the river, and down Chicago Avenue to the Lawson YMCA. I was home by ten. Max had left a note under

Love Underground © 2017 Owen Keehnen

Published by Out Tales Publishing

Cover Art by Adrian Nicholas

Love Underground:
The Clint and Joseph Diaries, 1962.

By Owen Keehnen

Used bookstores have always been a passion of mine. The thrill of the search for unique volumes and rare titles has been something I've relished for years. I've been fortunate. Combing the shelves for treasures has often proven fruitful, but no used bookstore find has been greater than my chance discovery last weekend.

Saturday morning, I walked downtown and saw a tattered handmade sign in a bookshop window announcing a "spring cleaning" sale. The place looked like it could use one. I crossed the street and went inside. A bell above the door announced my entry into Epic Reads.

"We need to clear room," the man at the front desk croaked around his cigarette. He looked up from his newspaper and made a halfhearted gesture toward the overflowing shelves. He asked if I needed any help. Actually, he said, "You don't need any help, do you?"

I replied that I didn't.

A piece by Beethoven was playing on a radio in the back. A cat dozed nearby. I wandered the stacks and was looking through a pile of mostly mysteries when something by Agatha Christie fell to the floor. As I bent to pick it up, I saw several notebooks piled at the bottom corner of the shelf. I picked one up and recognized at once that it was a diary. I supposed it was part of an estate sale or something dropped off in a box of books. The thought of exploring the contents intrigued me. I loved peeking into the plotless everyday lives of people and seeing what they did and what they thought when they believed no one was listening. Finding diaries in a used bookstore was not as rare as one would imagine.

The man at the front desk sold me the notebook for fifty cents. "I'm clearing room for new things," he repeated, lighting another cigarette. I handed him two quarters and put the composition book in my backpack. He laughed that he didn't care about the tax. "But I didn't say that," he added with a good-natured look over the top of his glasses.

Eager to explore the notebook's contents, I decided against walking downtown and instead took the Clark Street bus heading north. I fought the urge to begin reading on the bus ride home. I had something different in mind.

When I got home, I put a kettle on the stove, lay down on the couch, and opened the journal.

my door asking if I was free, but it was marked six thirty. I figured he'd made other plans by then. Max was quite popular.

Ray down the hall asked if I wanted to come by the TV room. I told him I was tired, but I think he knew I was giving him the air. Sometimes, I just like being alone. That isn't a crime. Retail is enough social interaction for me for the day. I ended up reading *The Carpetbaggers* by Harold Robbins until almost two a.m. Boy, but I could hear the carrying-on next door. Not that they were so loud, but it gets real quiet around here that time of night, and my ears pick up at that sort of doings. Made it tough for a fellow to fall asleep.

Tuesday April 10

Woke up late this morning and never quite caught up all day. So many people can get away with being late now and again, but I can never do that. Just the way I was raised. My ethic. Always wonder if they are looking for a reason to let me go.

Sophia Loren is all over the news for winning an Oscar for *Two Women*. *West Side Story* was the big winner at the Academy Awards last night. I forgot it was on. Big party in the TV room, I heard. That was what Ray was referring to. I thought he was just being a pest. Not that I think of him that way.

Made it to work with two minutes to spare. Never been that close before. Usually I have time for a cup of coffee or a cigarette before undraping my counter. Floor manager was just coming around when I dashed behind it and stowed the cloth. A moment later, he came back with a new fellow. Bob's replacement? He was certainly younger, probably still in his mid-twenties. The young man had an athletic build and square jaw. Quite handsome. Ella will go gaga over this one and probably already has. The new man smiled and nodded my way as he passed my counter. Very civil of him, I thought.

Slow day. Sold some new ties and hats for Easter. Annoyed by a woman who wanted her purchases wrapped. Then told me to hurry it up and stop fussing, and then proceeded to inspect my handiwork. We can't say anything except, "Yes, ma'am." I smiled through it all and bit my lip until it bled. At the end of the day, those annoyances are what remains. The squeaky wheel and all that. Maybe people wouldn't be so rude if they knew that, or maybe it wouldn't matter. Maybe they like to be remembered. Listened to. Noticed. Many people are rude to us simply because they know they can be.

A steam with a bit of horseplay in the evening downstairs. Max was there. He winked and asked if I got his note. I said I did. We ended the conversation right there. I said we'd have plenty of time to talk later. The Lawson is a magnet for that sort of goings-on and is safer than the bars. I don't like the thought of a bar because someone might see me coming or going. Usually I need to have a few drinks under my belt to step foot inside. Raids. Lavender sweeps. Daley wants none of that mischief in Chicago, at least around election time. That when the vice squad gets really busy. The parks can be unsafe. Not only because of undercover officers, they're also frequented by hooligans. Last month, I went to one of the bathhouses downtown, but it was during the day. Mostly empty and largely depressing. After a while I got what I was looking for. Truth be told, it was less adventurous than the Lawson. Maybe I was just hungry for something different. Excitement. I get that way sometimes. I think we all do.

Wednesday April 11

Surprising start to the day. Heading to the showers this morning, and who do I see walking back but Clint, that handsome new fellow at work. He was only wearing a towel. He said, "Hey, don't you work at M_____?" I said yes and introduced myself as Joseph Hoagland, Men's Ties and Hats. I was mortified I'd added my department. He just smiled. I didn't know what more to say, not having brushed my teeth. I was so intimidated by the sheer beauty of this young man, especially clothed only in a towel. Clint has a wonderful physique, plates and bulges of muscle, almost like a hirsute Mickey Hargitay. Clearly, he works out with weights or is some sort of physical culture devotee. He was very defined without being bulky.

Afterward I worried my eyes had betrayed me. Revealed my desire.

Clint said he would see me later at work. When I told him it was my day off, he winked and said, "Lucky you." His room at the Lawson is actually just three doors down from mine on the other side of the hall. He's right next to Ray. I suspect we'll be seeing a lot of one another. The thought makes me both excited and nervous. I wonder if he knows the sort of thing that goes on around here. With his looks and physique, he'll find out soon enough. I worry he might bring the information back to my coworkers at M_____ and say, "That Joseph lives there right in the *middle of it* all and has for years. He doesn't seem to mind. That must mean he fancies having perverts around and that sort of thing." Eyebrows would rise. Nods of agreement. "Birds of a feather," they'd all say. Appliances and Housewares would have a field day.

My neighbor to the right, Frankie, was a witness to the exchange. He just smiled and said, "Oh my." Frankie is very flamboyant. When he takes a shower, he wears a torso towel like a woman, with cloth covering both his breasts and his genitals. Sometimes he even fashions a second towel as a turban. He's so outrageous I'm amazed he can hold a job, but he works at one of the gay bars around Division. Max said he has quite a following there. *He's notorious.*

Dinner with my brother, David, and his wife, Simone. We went to the Cafe De Paris in the Dearborn Park Hotel. Simone did most of the talking. She's like a windup toy that way. I think it comes from being alone all day. Or maybe I make her nervous. She's very sweet and entertaining, but she can be draining. Don't know how David stands it day in and day out. Maybe she's silent around him.

When I came home, I half expected to see Clint in the hallways but didn't. Wandered down to the TV room and watched *The Dick Van Dyke Show* then went to my room and finished *The Carpetbaggers*. Need to pick up something new tomorrow during my lunch break.

Thursday April 12

Work was taxing. Clint was there and said hello. Rumor is he's a temporary hire and his family has connections. Ella whispered he was hired as a *favor*. Management had the poor kid running around all day. They test all the new workers that way, even the "connected" ones, I guess. Clint carried on with a smile. He's already learned how to play the game. Good-natured. He seems like a fine young man, and people seem especially eager to get on his good side. I think he will work out well at M_____.

Slow day, so it was a good time to restock and clean my counter displays. I've never been one for idleness, so standing and smiling and constantly anticipating can sometimes be hard. Nothing to do sends my mind wandering. Never a good thing. Management doesn't like us to think of other things. Management likes us to remain focused. Attentive. Ready to serve. They send in secret shoppers to make sure we're always proper ambassadors of M_____.

The Housewares fellows were at it again today. They are so unprofessional at times. So large for attention. I cannot imagine being that unfettered and assured of your place in the world. They fit into the norm with their wives and their broods of children, so they can behave that way. The world gives them permission and encouragement to be who they are. Those fellows have no comprehension of caution or secretiveness or any world aside from their own. They see only one sort of life. I view that world from outer space while living in another one altogether.

The need to be constantly vigilant makes me resentful. My world can be thrilling, but the burden is in its fragility and the fear of discovery. My life can be shattered with one indiscretion. Public shaming in the papers. Living open, as some do, means being an outcast. I've never been that brave. I was raised to be a solid member of society. Upstanding rather than outstanding. A part rather than apart. I do what most of us do. I blend, seeking invisibility and leading a secret life in the shadows. *A confirmed bachelor. A loner who never met the right girl.* The social pressure eases, eventually. In time, most people start to see you as sexless because they can't imagine anything else. I shouldn't complain. Ignorance makes an ideal camouflage. Sometimes I'm tempted to shock them. Sometimes I think, *If they only knew.* They only see one side of the world and so little of mine. Their vision hasn't adjusted to perceive anything else.

This evening I went to the TV room to watch *Dr. Kildare.* Half the guys in the Lawson are in love with Richard Chamberlain. And why shouldn't they be?

Friday April 13

Friday the 13th was anything but bad luck. Things are rarely in accord with their reputations. At the store Clint came by my counter and asked if I wanted to have lunch with him. A flabbergasted and fumbling yes. I'm sure I blushed. I worried about being too enthusiastic, too obvious. But he seemed genuine.

We sat on the grass in Grant Park and had our sandwiches and soda pops. As I lit a cigarette he unbuttoned his shirt and lay back on the grass. Chest plates. Broad. Firm. Very Hairy. Very. A hairy chest attracts me every time. So masculine. Virile. The sun beat down upon him. Both of us lightly sweating—Clint from the heat of the sun and me from the heat of watching him. His eyes were closed, and he had a smile on his face. He rubbed his hand across his strong chest. Absently. I wished so much it was my hand. I was lost in the fantasy when he finally turned, shielded his eyes from the sun, and said, "Springtime nineteen sixty two is here, my friend."

Indeed it was. The way he said it disarmed me. There was such beauty in it, such pure chumminess that I immediately felt at ease and lay back upon the grass as well. Clint is quite winning. A thoroughly engaging young man. We had to step lively to make it back to the store on time. Boy, but Clint took me out of my skin and made me feel twenty years younger. I usually eat alone in the lunchroom, using an open novel as my shield. I enjoyed being with this young man, but I didn't want to make a fool of myself. Mustn't forget my head. None of us in this position can afford to be that careless.

After work, he asked if I was going back to the Lawson. I said I had planned on it, but in a way that made it clear I was open for something else. He asked if I wanted to walk home, and I made some cornball comment about getting my daily exercise, which made me sound about a hundred and five years old. He said he'd meet me out front at ten past five. And at 5:10 there he was, no tricks, no shenanigans. *Alone*. We talked while walking home in the sunshine. He's twenty-two and from the North Shore. Wilmette. *Posh*. Wanted to get out from under his family's name and make good in the world. Sounds like his father is quite the muckety-muck. I admire Clint wanting to emerge from that shadow. He shows a good amount of character. He has captivated me. His maturity is blended with flashes of boyish charm. *Refreshing*. I wish Clint had come along twenty years ago, even ten. Life had more possibilities then. As it stands, I'm old enough to be his father. Perhaps that is part of my appeal.

On the way home, he asked if I wanted to stop off someplace and have a beer. What choice did I have? There was no saying No. Instead I said "Sure." Smitten by this fine young man, I'd already given myself over to anything Clint might suggest. Over beer and cigarettes, we talked some more. I said I was forty-two and I'd been at M_____ for almost fifteen years. He asked if I liked it there. I said it was a fine place to work. He smiled and said I didn't answer whether I liked it or not. He didn't say it to be rude, but his youth makes being somewhere that is "just okay" for fifteen years seem almost obscene. Maybe he's right. Maybe it is obscene.

After our second round of beers, Clint said he had to get back. He wanted to work out. As we walked in the front doors of the Lawson YMCA, he said, "You should come down, and we could work out together." Boy, I didn't know what to say. The thought was simultaneously frightening and exciting. I did have the necessary athletic clothing. I worried about revealing myself, but knew I would regret declining his invitation. I told him that would be fine. Fine? Ugh! Said I would meet him in the weight room in a half hour. He asked why so long. I said I had things to do. Mostly that entailed wanting to get all this down in my journal. Now I am lying here in my gym clothing, readying myself to meet him in the weight room in five more minutes. Friday the 13th, unlucky indeed! Be still my beating heart.

The evening with Clint was better than I could have imagined. So appealing in his weightlifting outfit. He is Hercules and hayseed and North Shore combined. I admired his muscles as they twitched and pulsed and shone with sweat. Longed to bury my face in the perspiration stains on his shirt. To hold him close. To have him hold me close. I admire Clint's determination, his self-challenge to lift more. To improve himself. I had that at one time, but qualities fade if they go unnourished. Where had my need for self-betterment gone?

Clint's focus is exceptional. He motivated me to push harder. His encouragement and approval was everything. This gym partnership brought a physical closeness, something I usually reserved only for trysts. Clint's musky scent alone had me hypnotized. I'd never interacted like this with another man before. I had shied away from all athletics and sports as a youth.

Typically, I took my exercise through brisk walks or some solitary pursuit. Sometimes, I swam in the pool, but most physical exertion was merely a prelude to the sauna and the steam room. Exercise justified what I hoped would come later.

The weight room was all new territory, but Clint made me feel I belonged there. He is my glistening ticket of entry. Now that place is no longer foreign to me. Afterward, Clint said he was going to take a shower and a steam. I wondered if he knew what to expect. Things can get a bit playful in the showers and steam room, and Clint was a shiny new toy. The steam room was where I first met Max.

I was tempted to accompany Clint but feared I would lose control, terrified my attraction would betray me. Told him I needed to get back. He smiled and said no problem. He was already pulling his sweat-soaked shirt over his head. Big whiff of that musky scent. The broad expanse of his hirsute chest took my breath away. I said thanks again just as he pulled down his shorts. He stood in a white athletic supporter and absently reached down to scratch where the elastic dug into his thighs. I was pounding in my shorts and hoped my excitement wasn't visible. I held my sweat towel before me. Stammered. Mustn't stare. I came back to my room in a fever to relieve myself. That beautiful body. A sweet and genuine young man. Gentle yet strong. His rapt attention on me, Joseph. Me. Afterward, I lay spent, wondering and tinged with regret. I should have taken a steam with him.

An hour later, when I went to the bathroom down the hall, I saw Clint coming back from the gym. His back was as beautiful as the rest of him, broad and tapering to a trim waist. He didn't see me. He was already halfway to his room. I wonder if he was in the showers and steam room the entire time. A long time to just steam, especially around here. Maybe that was part of his personal athletics routine. But usually around here that means extra activity. Maybe that's wishful thinking on my part. In all the time we spent together, he never once mentioned a girlfriend or even commented on the attributes of any female. Don't most men do that sort of thing?

Later.

I tried to read a bit before I went to sleep, but not even John O'Hara's *From The Terrace* could keep my mind off Clint. Eventually, I succumbed to my desire. In my fantasy, we went in the steam room together and slyly exposed ourselves to one another. The mutual interest was obvious. I imagined holding him in my arms and taking his manhood into my mouth. I felt his excitement rise and begin to peak. I felt the twitch and expansion of him. I heard the guttural moan of his release. As I imagined his seed going down my throat, I felt the explosion of pleasure in my hand. The daydream fulfilled me like no other in recent memory. Oftentimes, my fantasies are about my oppressors. Sad but true. With Clint, it was something else entirely. There was sex, but there was more. With Clint, it was about being together more than just physically. I fell asleep with a smile on my face. I imagined my smile as a duplicate of the one he wore as he lay back on the grass earlier in the day.

Saturday April 14

Busy day at work, but more browsers than buyers. Lots of refolding. Rearranging. Some decent sales. The gents are getting prepared for Easter. Had a man get snippy because I couldn't wait on him immediately. Told me later he was a minister and should not have to wait. He failed to see the irony in the situation. Even referred to himself as a Man of God. One simply has to smile and apologize through it all. So demeaning.

Today the weather turned cooler, so I took the subway home. Train service was slow. The cars were very crowded. Everyone seemed out today. We were packed in like sardines. Thankfully, the Lawson is only four stops down the line.

When I got home, I debated for about a minute whether to head to the weight room before changing and heading down to the gym. My behavior seemed transparent. Desperate. Didn't matter. No Clint. Perhaps he's gone for the weekend. He didn't mention anything to me on Friday, but then, why would he? He owed me nothing. I need to keep things in perspective and not be such a fool.

Lots of holding stares in the exercise area. These men had a good idea of how they wanted to spend their Saturday nights. Played a bit with a man in the steam room until the heat and the smell of solvent made me queasy. Shouldn't have let myself get so dehydrated. The man asked if I wanted to go to a bar later. I could tell by the way he said it that he meant *that* kind of bar. I mentioned those places being dangerous and said they were all mob owned. He said not all of them, then joked that the only thing I had to worry about at the Gold Coast was myself. I'd heard of it. The Gold Coast was a gay biker bar. I declined. He said too bad, some *very* interesting things go on there. He took the towel from about his waist and draped it over his shoulders as he left the steam room. He looked back and smiled when he saw me watch him leave. I was a fool not to join him.

Sunday April 15

Clint must have gone away for the weekend. Though I've only known him a brief time, it's still strange not to see him here or at work. Foggy out today. Read a bit of the O'Hara book, then went to shop for socks. A couple of my old pair were worn in the heel. I should have bought them at work since I receive a healthy discount, but I abhor stepping foot in the door if I have the day off. Part of me likes being a bit devious by shopping at the competition. Makes me feel like less a slave of M_____.

Later. Went down to the workout room, and there he was. Clint said he had to go to Wilmette for a wedding. He said it was a high school friend. He pointed to the barbells and smiled. "I have to work off that fancy cake." Could he be any more adorable? I asked if everyone had asked him when he was getting married. He just nodded and rolled his eyes. That would have been an ideal time for him to mention a girlfriend, a sweetheart, anything. Clint said nothing. I was going to ask if he took a date but thought better of it. I didn't want to cause an eye roll. I wanted to be different. Sometimes talking to young people can be so hard.

He was just finishing his workout. I said I had come down for a quick bit of exercise. Fifteen minutes. *Better than not coming at all*, I said. Ten of those minutes spent talking to him. *So transparent. Obvious.* Who was I fooling? He headed into the locker room, and I followed. We grabbed towels on the way. My heart was pounding.

At his locker, he pulled his sweat-soaked T-shirt over his head and took a whiff of it before tossing it in. So beautiful—if I've said it before, pardon me, but this bears repetition—his broad chest with fanning hair that narrowed to a trail down his flat stomach was nothing less than breathtaking. Every inch of him was stunning. I admired his broad back, the veins in relief along his biceps, the apparent power of his shoulders. He looked like a model from one of the *Physique* magazines.

I took the locker directly across from him and undressed slowly, telling some asinine story about work. He dropped his shorts and jock in one swift move. I caught a flash of firm, furry buttocks as he headed for the shower area. I didn't want to seem like I was following him, so I ducked into the steam room. *I was crazed.* I broke something up when I entered. Three men walked from the center of the room and into three opposite corners.

A moment later, Clint stuck his head in. "Hey, nice chatting with you, Joseph. I am heading back to my room. I've got some things to do." I couldn't help but notice the way his towel hung low across his hips and the muscled vee above his pubis. When Clint saw one of the men in the cloud of steam, he nodded. It was Max! I wondered how they knew each other. Max and I were *friendly*, well - more than friendly I suppose, but I didn't want to violate some sort of gentleman's code by asking how he knew Clint. Having sex was one thing, but sharing the carnal details about a partner was something else entirely. That sort of talk could cause a lot of problems.

Clint came to my room a couple hours later. He was wearing a tight white T-shirt and boxers. Wow. So many bulges to tempt my eyes. I tried not to look, but I'm sure I did. Clint leaned against the doorframe and asked when I was heading to work in the morning.

I said I would probably leave around seven thirty and added, "I like to get there early." He asked me if I wanted to walk over together. I said sure.

"Then it's a date," he said, smiling.

Does he realize the effect his words have on me?

Clint is going to come by my room tomorrow. Boy, but I am heading to sleep with a smile on my face tonight. The image of him in that doorway was like glimpsing the gates of heaven. I was *trembling*. The bulge in his boxers. The bulge of his biceps. The T-shirt stretched taut across his chest. The hair peeking out from his collar. The high curve of his buttocks as he turned to leave. Perfection.

Inexplicably, Clint seems fond of me, but I don't know in what way. Is this an innocent friendship to him? I don't want to misinterpret things. At the same time, so many opportunities have slipped by me in the past, lost chances for what may have been happiness. Maybe not lasting happiness, but happiness nonetheless. Too many times I've worried about looking foolish and being foolish. I've been too cautious. Older and wiser can mean so many things. *Lacking nerve*. I don't want to lose my chance with Clint out of fear, and I don't want to jeopardize our friendship. I want him so badly. Part of me feels he's the sort who is worth risking my pride, worth risking everything. I've certainly been a fool for less.

I'll wait for a sign.

Monday April 16

Horrible news. Clara Blandick who played Auntie Em in *The Wizard of Oz* committed suicide yesterday at age eighty-four. Death is so odd. I think of some of those who've died recently—Ernie Kovacs, Marion Davies, Barry Fitzgerald, and others. So many of my beloved film and TV folk dying. They have kept me company for hours and still do when I go to the TV room for the late show.

Clint and I took lunch break together again today. We walked over to the park and stretched out on the grass and let the sun beat down upon us. That warmth felt terrific. Clint unbuttoned his shirt again. Touched himself again. I smoked and tried not to stare. Does he realize the effect he has on me? The depth of my desire?

Being there with him felt so ideal. Lying there, just talking. Heck, it would have been ideal if this was twenty years ago, and I was lying there with someone my own age. Clint picked a bit of grass and threw it on my chest. *Flirtation?* I must have been dozing by then. The slight tickle of the grass startled me. I brushed the blades aside and bolted upright. Clint teased that I talked in my sleep. At least I hoped that he was teasing. If that was true, Lord knows what I could have said. Maybe if I was unconscious, I'd finally have the courage to express what I felt.

Had a horrible thought later—maybe the guys from Appliances and Housewares had gotten to Clint first and this was all part of some elaborate prank, a ruse to make me look foolish and reveal my secrets. Fear of ridicule can take me to the darkest places. *Irrational places.* Trust has never been my strong suit. Is the thought that Clint might have romantic feelings for me so inconceivable? Sure, I'm forty-two, but I'm relatively handsome. Trim. Fit. I've been compared to Dana Andrews. I'm not entirely ancient. Not successful financially, though I have managed to save up a good amount of money, mostly as the result of frugal living. Saving is easier without reason to splurge. I have some money invested and a solid savings account.

If I wasn't a confirmed bachelor, I'd be considered a decent catch. Why should it be so different in the world of men? Maybe because instead of being pressured to come together, like people in the heterosexual world, there is only a repellent pull to keep us apart. I may be a good catch, but would I be worth the risk? Who is worth that price? Choosing me in that way would mean choosing much more than just choosing me. Choosing another man would mean choosing courage and defiance and choosing to be an outsider. Very few are that brave or that in love. I like to think I might be capable under ideal circumstances, but circumstances of that sort are never ideal. There are always complications. Always.

Tuesday April 17

I did something so foolish. *Idiot!* Usually, I exercise greater caution. After work yesterday, I walked to that little bar where Clint and I stopped the day we walked back to the Lawson. I sat there and had one beer after another until I was soused. Sitting there on the barstool, I decided I could not take another day with all this uncertainty. I asked the bartender for a six-pack to go and made my way back here. No alcohol allowed, so I needed to smuggle it past the front desk beneath my raincoat. I'd never done that before. Turns out the person at the front desk didn't much care.

Deciding I needed to be honest with the object of my affection, I sat down and wrote Clint a letter. Drafts and more drafts of the letter were crumpled and tossed beside the bed when I awoke this morning. Based on the last balled-up version by the desk, the final letter probably went something like this:

Dear Clint,
This is Joseph. I feel an urgent need to write this letter to let you know how I have been feeling. Perhaps you are already aware, but my uncertainty over the issue has become unbearable. Clint, I find you a very attractive, industrious, and level-headed young man, and I deeply enjoy the time we spend together. In fact, I would like to spend more time with you. If this is not something you wish to do, for whatever reason, there are certainly no hard feelings. I just wanted you to know that

the friendship we have is something that I hold in high regard.

    Yours Truly,
    Joseph

I cringe at the thought of writing those words. What seemed a great idea on a barstool is in fact, imbecilic. I didn't even really tell him what I was feeling anyway. *I enjoy spending time with you?* What is he supposed to make of a note like that? I slipped the finished note beneath his door at God knows what hour. If he did think of me in a romantic way, the schoolmarm tone and phrasing of my note is certain to dampen his ardor. *I'm such an oaf.* Somehow, I managed to write something incriminating, yet unclear and boring at the same time.

I'm tempted to run to his room to try to retrieve the note from beneath his door. It's quarter after ten. Ugh. Clint is working today. He would have seen it a couple hours ago when he was getting ready. He seems like a discreet young man, but how can I know? I've never known him to be in possession of something like this. He is young. He might say something or show someone. Then where will I be? Why couldn't I have left well enough alone?

I remembered Max in the steam room and Clint's familiar hello. Although I would never inquire about someone's sexual encounters, I needed to know. Maybe Max knew something I didn't. I went down to the gym and took a steam. I was sweating and drinking cup after cup of water. My hangover was gone in about an hour. Men came and went, but there was no action. Eventually Max came in. Nothing has happened between us in weeks. We're more friends than anything. We talked about this and that. Max was talking about the latest Belle Barth album and how he thought she was the funniest woman alive. He saw her last year someplace on Rush Street. I never worked up the nerve to ask about Clint. Heck, I figured I would find out soon enough anyway. Finally, I came back upstairs and took a nap. I was exhausted and fell into a sleep deeper than dreaming and awoke a full two hours later.

Now I lie here, famished from not eating all day and worried that if I leave the room to get something to eat, I'll run into Clint. He should be home from work soon. Maybe I'll wait another hour or so before venturing out. Even going to the bathroom at the end of the hall seems incredibly risky. I know I'll see him eventually, and I'll have to explain the note. I just don't want eventually to be now... or anytime soon. I work tomorrow, but I can't remember if Clint said he was scheduled. This entire day has been frittered away on foolishness and regret.

I hate not being in control of a situation.

Wednesday April 18

Well, I endured last night. Writing this on lunch break. Rainy. Humid. Unseasonably warm. No Clint at work. Still no response from the letter. Those guys in Appliances and Housewares are being jerks again. No surprises there. Those fools are always looking for ammunition. I fear they'll somehow get their hands on the letter. I doubt Clint would do something like that, but people can act awfully strange when confronted with my sort. Scenarios go from bad to worse in my mind. Paranoia runs amok. Just wish I'd never said a word. One of the first rules of this underground is to never put anything in writing. Ever. Wise men are often undone by foolish acts. Even as I write that, I realize that's not always the case. Rules are meant to be bent and sometimes broken. Sometimes love, or something like it, is worth the risk. I refuse to make love the enemy.

When I got home, I found a note slipped beneath my door. It was written on the flip side of the note I sent Clint.

Joseph -
Yes, I would like that. I enjoy your company as well. Want to work out tonight? I am heading down there around 5:30.
Clint.

The note is puzzling in its brevity and provides absolutely no answers. At least our friendship appears unshaken, which relieves me. Nothing catastrophic occurred. No bolts of lightning or police banging at the door. The note was not the seed of my undoing... and it was back in my possession. Once again my imagination has proven to be an unreliable and hysterical source. You'd think I'd be wise to that by age forty-two. *But no*.

Getting ready to head to the gym area now. The note is vague, but hopefully Clint's behavior will provide some clues, if not some answers.

Boy, but everything has changed. Clint understands the note. He knows what I was trying to say and why I sidestepped saying it outright. *He knows*. And what's more, he feels the same connection. He told me he is attracted to older gentlemen, men of "my generation." That is confusing in some ways since I wonder if he is attracted to me or to people like me. Sometimes I need to slap myself. Feeling this happy makes me want to find things to worry about.

Clint explained everything as we progressed through our workout. Discussing these issues between sets was easier than sitting down face to face. Less intense. Doing it this way also made it very arousing. The smell of Clint, the hushed and intimate stating of our mutual attraction, the sharing of our feelings, whisperings and looks, sweating together, the physicality, all of it amounted to some heady foreplay. After our final set, Clint suggested we return to my room. We did.

I had fantasized about this night dozens of times, yet the consummation was even greater than the fantasy. He is so strong, so beautiful and sensitive, with soft skin covered by so much hair. Adventurous as a lover. *Playful. Open*. More experienced than I supposed. That was apparent as soon as he took me in his arms and kissed up the side of the neck to my mouth. He was aggressive and yet gentle. He knew what was coming and wanted to savor it. The sign of a confident lover. He had reason to be. I ache to recall his prowess.

Afterward, he collapsed upon me. His weight was a wonderful slab of security, pinning me to this perfect moment. I felt his heart beating against mine. We didn't shower after our workout. The heady scent of sweat and sex filled the room. Permeated my skin.

I grabbed a cigarette from the pack on the desk and asked Clint if he wanted one. He declined with a smile and turned with his head propped on his hand. I said I quit for the most part, but still had one or two a day.

Clint said he knew, I'd smoked in front of him before. Then he asked how old I was. He smiled when I told him. Forty-two and twenty-two. That doesn't seem to bother him in the least. On the contrary, he seems amused. I asked him how long he has known he was this way, and he told me since forever. When he asked me, I said I've been aware of my attraction to men since I was twenty. By the time I snubbed out my smoke, Clint wanted to fool around again. Usually that would be a prime difference between our ages, but with Clint, I managed to rise to the occasion. With Clint, I have become twenty-two all over again. Youth by osmosis.

Thursday April 19

Loving the enormous inside joke we have on the world. Our divine and sublime secret. The big world out there has no idea.... doesn't suspect we have our own atmosphere, our own universe. The world sees us as friends, coworkers, and residents of the Lawson. They know so little. We're something more. Reality has changed completely. Yet to the outside world, nothing has changed. The world is oblivious. *Blind*. The thought makes me wonder if that is always the case. I considered the people I see on the bus or at the store or anywhere. Are many of them harboring delicious secrets and unsuspected worlds as well?

Are unseen miracles all around me everyday?

We walked to work today. We were mostly quiet in the best imaginable way. Strange how a comfortable silence can be so different from an uncomfortable one. We were blissful and at peace. Spring is here. You could feel it in the warmth and angle of the sunlight and in the breeze and in the periodic pop of color from budding flowers. The trees are set to explode. Wow! Potential is everywhere.

I don't know if everyone on the street was happy because the day was so lovely, or if the only thing that has changed is my attitude. Do others sense a difference as well? People smiled. People nodded. People walked with a spring in their step. Great music came from the passing cars. Heck, even the pigeons seemed to stop pecking their food as we went by. Everything was part of a grand orchestration. All was a part of my movie. Sometime during the walk, I realized this harmony I saw everywhere was love. The effect it had on the world was the purest sort of magic.

Work was another place altogether or at least in its proper perspective. For the first time, I was able to clearly see how little of this day-to-day drama matters. Clint and I eyed one another a couple times during the shift and shared a smile. My heart almost exploded. I could feel its eager leap in my chest. I think Clint was feeling the same. My customers seemed to fall under the same magical spell, and I met my weekly quota in a single day. No hassles, or the ones that occurred were of no consequence. Unpleasantries have no place in this new and spectacular world.

After work, Clint and I walked home and stopped at that little bar along the way, and then we stared at one another across the booth. I smoked over my quota for the day, and we drank longnecks. The jukebox played "I Fall to Pieces" by Patsy Cline, then Clint winked and said let's go back to the Lawson. We came back to my room and were feeling sleepy from the beers and the day, so we took a nap in each other's arms. We woke up around nine for a round of lovemaking. He held me tightly as he penetrated me. Whispering all the things I longed to hear. His sexual know-how made me curious as to his prowess. Clint said he'd had *friends* before. When I asked him who, he said, "just different guys." I didn't pry. Or I should say, I didn't pry *further*. His past was none of my business. He was back in his own room by midnight. If he had stayed, we never would have gotten to sleep.

I missed tonight's episode of *Dr. Kildare* on NBC, and I didn't care at all. I have something even better than Richard Chamberlain.

Friday April 20

Another great day. We were both off work. So nice. We worked out this morning, then decided to walk down the street to a diner for breakfast. Coffees and farmer breakfasts. "Heart attack on a plate" was what Clint called it. He can be very funny. Afterward, we decided to walk off a bit of the meal. The day was warm and sunny. Clint ended up carrying his windbreaker. We strolled down along the river and crossed over to the Loop. Along the way, I asked Clint what he wanted to do with his life. He is thinking about college. He said it hadn't worked out the first time, but now he needed to go. I asked what he meant, but I guess he didn't hear me.

He asked if I wanted to take in a matinee. We walked over to State Street. *Pit and the Pendulum* was on the marquee. Vincent Price and Edgar Allan Poe seemed a fun diversion. The movie was everything we hoped. We sat low in our seats and shared a popcorn and jumped at several startling parts of the movie. Like kids! The film was frightening, vibrant, and medieval at the same time. We both admitted Price's costar in the movie, John Kerr, is gorgeous. No one gave us a second glance.

The last time I was at this theater was a very different experience. I was no stranger to this underground. All sorts of doings went on up in the balcony. I was drawn to those darkened rows like a moth to a flame. Last time I was too busy watching the action in the theater to see any of the action on the screen. The film was something with Glenn Ford. The balcony was populated by a scattering of single men engaged in everything but the film. They were playing musical chairs. Coming together, moving apart, visiting the men's room together. This place hadn't been raided in months. Not since before the last election.

The balconies of the downtown theaters were proven spots to connect. A man got a blow job right at the end of the row. I wasn't bold enough for anything like that. The most I ever did was play a bit with a man at the urinals in the second-floor bathroom. I wonder if Clint knows about the stuff that occurs in the upper tiers of the movie houses. He didn't say a thing, but I doubt it was because he worried about appearing perverted. He doesn't seem to care how he comes across. Confidence to spare. I'd say it was youth, but I was never that confident at his age. As we crossed the lobby and approached the exit doors, I saw several men furtively taking the stairs to the balcony. I looked at Clint. Things were different now, but the notion of those encounters still held a certain appeal. Mostly curiosity.

Afterward, we came back to the Lawson. We were heading up to my room when the man at the front desk told Clint that he had visitors earlier. He said the people told him they'd be back in a few minutes. As soon as he said it, a well-dressed couple came back through the door. I could see Clint stiffen. He introduced them as his parents. His father looked somewhat familiar. Clint introduced me as "a guy who lives here."

"Oh," said his mother with a note of condescension, "I thought this place was for younger men." I wasn't sure if she meant to be rude, but she succeeded.

His father looked at me, then at Clint, and then back at me and said, "I see."

I suspect they both knew what was going on whether they cared to admit it or not. They were here to take Clint to dinner. Clint said he had forgotten they were coming today. He told them he was going to get changed and would be down in a few minutes. We took the stairs. On the climb to our floor, he told me how much he resented their coming here, "I moved here to get away." He said he wished they had just stayed in Wilmette. I said that maybe they just wanted to see him. He scoffed and said that was one way of looking at it. When I asked what he meant, he raised a hand as if to say never mind. His face was flushed. No one is objective when it comes to their family.

Clint said he'd come knock on my door when they got back from dinner.

12:00 midnight. He hasn't come by.

Saturday April 21

Today was an upsetting day, mostly because I never heard from Clint. He called in sick to work. I worried about what was going on, why his parents had come for a visit, and why he'd reacted in such a way when they appeared.

More spinning of dark scenarios.

At first I thought it was because of me, but I suspect there was something more. He was so well-mannered at all other times, his brusqueness took me aback. Maybe it had something to do with the men he had known before.

Even though we were busy at the store, my time behind the counter dragged. The Appliances and Housewares guys were ribbing me, trying to get a rise out of me, but I couldn't care less. *Idiots*. High school was so long ago. *Grow up*.

When I came back to my room, I walked down the hall and knocked on Clint's door. No answer. No sound is lonelier than the hollow unanswered knock on a lover's door. I came back here and tried to read. My mind was elsewhere. I walked down the street and had some Chinese food. I tossed a coin in the Buddha's lap for good luck. I asked for a sign. *A message*. An indication of what I should do. None was forthcoming. Empty wishes. Only yesterday I couldn't imagine wanting for anything more. Was I so needy that one day apart would cause such distress? Until that moment, I suppose I never realized how lonely I had really been.

The streets were packed with people. The crowds got on my nerves. There should be a separate sidewalk for tourists.

Sunday April 22

Still nothing from Clint. I slipped another note beneath his door. This one was in a sealed envelope just in case he came upstairs with his parents in tow. I went up on the roof for a bit and stretched out in the sunshine with my book. Easier to get a tan when you're twenty-four floors closer to the sun. The roof always reminds me of a movie set. Surreal. Panoramic Chicago view. The neon YMCA sign is even more impressive after dark. Coming on to the roof after dusk is not allowed, but plenty of men break the rule for a bit of romance under the stars. So many of us who live here are romantics at heart... wanting love so badly and feeling love so deeply. Willing to risk everything for it.

People have jumped to their deaths from up here. I have heard a suicide happens here almost every season, but I've never seen one. I've only heard the whispers. *That blond guy on the third floor, the one who always wore the green windbreaker, jumped off the roof on Saturday night. Kept mostly to himself.* That was the way obituaries were in the underground. Whispered. Even death seems a vague rumor. Plenty of John Does among our kind. Suicide often seems the only solution for a beaten-down and kicked-around romantic. *The disillusioned. The exiled.* Disowned by family and abandoned by love. I understand. Sometimes the loneliness can be unbearable. I've been on the figurative ledge myself. I've seen oblivion and eternity over the tips of my shoes. Curiosity has saved me more than anything else.

After a half hour lying out in the sun on the roof, I couldn't concentrate. Lots of frisky men roaming the Lawson today. Lots of cruising going on in the hallways. Several doors were partially open. Inhabitants lying invitingly on their beds. Dioramas of desire. I suppose it's the call of spring. At another time, I might have crossed a threshold or two. Gone inside and closed the door behind me and battled my loneliness with a partner. I had done that sort of thing before, plenty of times. Not today. Not since meeting Clint. Sex is nice, but it isn't what this is about. Sounds corny, but sex has become an expression more than a thrill or a release.

I came back to my room and closed the door and fantasized that Clint was beside me. I imagined every inch of his body. Felt the need of his manhood and saw the kindness in his eyes. My arms imagining the broad expanse of his shoulders. Hands braced on hips as he entered me. His mouth on mine. The scratch of his stubble. His sweat and his whispers and his moans. His shortening breath as it synchronized with mine. The fantasy was impossible to deny. I arched my back. Release with a smile before a brief but heavy sleep.

When I awoke, I walked down to the corner diner for a burger. Clint was still on my mind. Where could he be? Why hadn't he contacted me? Maybe his parents took him home for the weekend.

I came back to the Lawson and was feeling restless. Max came by and convinced me to come to his room. We listened to the Belle Barth album. She is hilarious, and so dirty. Frankie was there, practically in hysterics! Loved when she said to a woman in the crowd, "I was built like you by the time I was nine years old. My nipples are bigger than your tits." Afterward we listened to Frances Faye.

Monday April 23

Clint was not at work today. He took a personal day. When I came home, I found the note he'd slipped beneath my door, saying that he came by the Lawson to pick some things up from his room. He would be back tomorrow. He said he missed me and apologized, saying there is just a lot going on right now. He wrote, "See you at work," which meant we weren't walking to M_____ together. I read the note a dozen times and interpreted it a dozen different ways. Dark fears. The heart can make clarity of thought impossible.

I went down to the gym to take my mind off of things. That didn't work. I needed some sort of distraction. I ended up meeting a man named Paul and going back to his room. So much for my pristine new view of sex. We started playing around, and boy, I wanted to tell him that this was a mistake. That there was someone else. But it just grew too awkward to stop. Even in this underground, we abide by certain codes of honor. Instead of putting an end to things with Paul, I went through with it and felt awful afterward. During, actually. Paul was a nice man, but boy, he must think I'm a real screwball. Ugh! At least Paul is just staying here for work and will be leaving in a few days. Hope I don't run into him again.

Still worried about Clint and what tomorrow will bring.

I thought about going down to the TV room but decided against it. I wish Jack Paar was still hosting *The Tonight Show*.

Tuesday April 24

I sure am nervous.

Didn't see Clint much during the morning, but he came by my counter around eleven and asked if I wanted to go for lunch. I was so happy and said sure, keeping it cool because I knew people are always watching and listening. He came by to pick me up at noon. We walked over to Grant Park. We bought sandwiches on the way and lay on the grass. Another sunny day. This spring has been glorious in so many ways. We made small talk before lying back to feel the sun on our faces. I could see he was nervous by the rise and fall of his chest. Shortened breaths. Rather than simply enjoying the sun, I suspected Clint was lying on his back so he wouldn't have to look me in the eye while speaking. That was when he told me the news.

Last year, he received a draft notice. A Selective Service Order came, and he was to report for the Armed Forces Physical Exam. He said he should have expected it, given who his father was. I had no idea what that meant, but I didn't want to interrupt. He said he'd panicked at the time. Wanting anything but Army life, he enrolled in college to escape the military. Clint said he wasn't a good student and spent most of his time carousing around Pittsburgh.

"I didn't want to be there, either. College was the lesser of two evils as far as I was concerned." He flunked out of school. As a result, Clint was scheduled to appear on June 1, 1962 in Waukegan for his physical exam.

He'd convinced his parents to let him spend his final months in the city rather than Wilmette. He wanted to live a little before he went into the service. They had relented. His mother was hysterical over it all, but North Shore hysterical. When I asked Clint what that meant, he said, "Exercise and clothes, diet pills and cocktails." He said it to be funny, but boy, I wasn't laughing. I was already counting the days in my head. The thought of Clint leaving took my breath away.

I told Clint he could evade the draft by mentioning his attraction to men. He shielded his eyes from the sun and looked my way like I was insane. His look spoke volumes. He told me he'd sooner be at the front lines than have something like that on his record. "'Dishonorable' is not a word in my family's vocabulary," he said. I told him people had done it before. I said there was no shame in what I felt for him. He didn't see things the same way. "My parents would never go for that. My father would kill me and then have a coronary. My mother would die of shame. "They consider homosexuality the equivalent of being a communist."

Clint said his father was scrambling to get him in a college somewhere. "At least that's what he claims. But with his connections, he could do something. He doesn't want to. He has ulterior motives. He thinks the Army will toughen me up, make a man out of me."

Clint said he didn't care what happened anymore.

I wanted to tell him that hurt my feelings. I thought what we had shared should at least shake him of his indifference. I suspect he noticed my expression because two seconds later he revised his words. "It's not that I don't care, I'm just overwhelmed."

"Will you be sent to Korea?"

He didn't know, though he had heard that troops were starting to be sent to Vietnam as well. "This is all over a month away. I don't want to think about it. Not now, anyway. I just want our time together."

I loved him even more for saying that. I reached for his hand. He saw it out of the corner of his eye. If things had been different and this world was a bit more tolerant, he would have taken my hand. But eyes were everywhere. *We were a threat to the American way of life*. Instead, I pulled my hand back, and Clint dug his fingers into the grass.

If only…

I picked a dandelion head and then another and tossed them on his chest. If all we have is six weeks together, then I am determined to make these six weeks terrific. Military service is not forever. If we are meant to be, we can weather this storm. Greater hardships are endured every day.

We were a half hour late returning from lunch. The floor manager welcomed Clint back to work with a thin smile. Displeased but silent. He took great satisfaction in telling me not to make tardiness a habit and that my time sheet would be adjusted accordingly. Clint's family must be very well connected to escape his pettiness.

Wednesday April 25

Today Clint and I spent the morning in my room making love and talking. *Ideal.* If nuclear war with Russia happens and the warhead is launched, this is where and how I would like to spend my remaining hours. If the communists take over and attempt to rob us of our memories, good luck. A morning of making love to Clint will be a tough memory to take from me.

Eventually, we changed into shorts and went up to the roof to lie out in the sun. Clint is already quite tan. He said he has some Italian blood in him. Clint had several admirers among the sunbathers. I certainly can understand their interest. Clint really does have a perfect physique, though truth be told, that is not what I love about him. Physical beauty is a part of him, but it's not him. We have this chemistry and share a level of comfort that makes everything flow.

After an hour, I began to redden, so we changed and walked around downtown for a while. We went to see *Cape Fear*. Terrific thriller! Gregory Peck and Robert Mitchum are top-notch in it. There was a second feature, and we were feeling a little frisky, but rather than go back to the room, I took Clint by the hand and led him to the balcony. In the flickering light, our hands were in one another's lap. Unzipping. Fumbling. That familiar grip. Spit. Stroking while some inane *husband-plotting-to-kill-his-philandering-wife-who-isn't-cheating-at-all* suspense story unfolded upon the screen. The booming melodramatic score cloaked the sound of our doings.

Moans. The blessed friction. Clint ejaculated on my hand. I brought my fingers to my lips. Tangy. I want every bit, every drop of Clint. I smiled at him as I licked each digit dry. I said I needed coffee to go with his cream.

"You idiot." He laughed and shook his head.

That's how it is with us. Despite our differences, it's easy. Relaxed. Uninhibited.

We went to the Cordova Diner on the corner and ordered two cups of coffee and two pieces of blueberry pie. He asked how I came to Chicago. He knew so little about me. I said I was born here in Logan Square, and my parents had been factory workers. He asked about them, and I told him I was orphaned a long time ago. Not quite sure why I said that, because even though my mother died when I was five, my father is still alive. I didn't mention my brother at all. Sometimes I fabricate things for no reason. Sometimes a lie is the truth. I don't feel as though I have family.

Clint said he loved his parents, but at the same time, he envied me. "Being an orphan would sure simplify things." Clint said he was an only child, and his parents were pushing him toward a career. "Not a job, a career. I don't want to think about that yet." He said they want him to be an engineer. *A promising occupation.* That pressure had already caused problems. Clint said he might not have flunked out in Pittsburgh if he'd been interested in what he was being taught. "Now look where I am," he added.

"Yes, look where you are." I reached across the table and brushed his hand. Holding it would have been foolhardy, but denial made the anticipation of touching later all the sweeter. I told Clint he was here with me right now. That was all that mattered. We finished our coffee and pie and walked back to the Lawson. Another perfect memory in the making.

Anticipation.

And rewards.

He stayed in my room until the first light of dawn.

The day was everything I have always wanted life to be, encapsulated perfection. Happiness is nothing more than spending time being with a perfect someone. Everything is magic. It's not the event or the outcome, it's the ingredients.

Despite the peace and the joy, the dread of Clint's selective service notice still lurks in my mind, giving an edge of anxiety to the perfection. Periodically throughout the day, I think, "This is finite." But everything is. Life is finite. That makes it even more precious. Call us foolhardy, but the future is something we consciously choose to ignore. Tomorrow has no meaning. Not yet. That's the way we have to live. We have to surrender to the beauty and perfection of those moments that we do have.

Thursday April 26

On the walk to work this morning, Clint gave me another doozy of a surprise and told me he is going away with his parents for ten days.

TEN DAYS!

Such a large portion of our time together. Apparently, he always takes a spring vacation with his folks. This year, they're going to Paris. He said they're leaving next week. Ten less days we can share. I was angry. Shocked. Why didn't he tell me earlier? He said he didn't want to upset me. Damn right. His agreeing to go feels like betrayal. Part of me wanted to ask if he could have declined, but I held my tongue.

Part of me just says the hell with him. But that part of me is a fool.

People at work are starting to take notice of the amount of time we spend together. A couple of people, of course the Housewares and Appliances guys, even started calling us the Bobbsey Twins. I could tell the comment bothered Clint. When I asked if he wanted to walk home together later, he said he was going to go out with a couple guys from work. I knew he meant Housewares. *Of all people*. No invitation for me to join him was attached, not that I would have accepted. I was angry. Betrayed. I covered my anger with a shrug. I've become an expert at masking what I feel.

If our relationship is going to work, we can't worry what other people think. A prime example of being older and wiser. I can't blame him for wanting what I once wanted. *To belong*. I still do, I suppose, but after so many years and much disappointment, I gave up hoping. Clint is only behaving the way I would've behaved at his age.

Yes, I am jealous.

Of his parents.

Of the guys in Housewares and Appliances.

Hating that he is away from me tonight. *With them*.

That he's going away with his parents for TEN days.

Then leaving for the armed forces in a few weeks.

I don't want to share our time with anyone.

Went to see the movie *State Fair* after work. Loved Ann-Margret. Bobby Darin and Pamela Tiffin were okay, Pat Boone is certainly handsome, in a bland sort of way. But he should stick to singing. I enjoyed seeing Alice Faye on the screen again. Haven't seen her in a picture in ages. The movie lifted my spirits. That was saying something since my mood was foul going into the theater.

Afterward, I decided to keep HIM waiting and went for Chinese food and had a couple beers at a pub around the corner after that. The place was full of seasoned drinkers. Everyone was sitting alone. One empty stool in between defined the boundaries.

When I got back to the Lawson, I knocked on his door. He still wasn't in. *Livid*.

I waited up for him and read. Good news is I finished John O'Hara's *From the Terrace*. Enjoyable. Ha! Used that phrase twice about things today, and it fits too. That's a good way to sum up most everything without Clint: enjoyable, pleasant, a fine way to pass time inoffensively. Frittering life away. When we are apart, the best that anything can be is a pleasant diversion.

When I'm with Clint, there is no diversion, With him, I'm right where I should be. With Clint at my side, I'm present and alive in a way I haven't been in years. Without him, I'm just biding time.

Friday April 27

Clint was at my door early this morning. I asked him why he was up so early. We didn't have to leave for work for another hour. *Exactly*, he said. He offered a wicked smile and pushed me back on the cot. Boy, but that's the way to start the day. After our fevered lovemaking, I remembered I was irked with him. He said all he could think about last night was wanting to be here with me, but those jokers from Housewares and Appliances had driven him to some honky-tonk in Oak Park. They wanted someplace out of the city where they could play Casanova and make time with girls. Disgusting. They're all married with children. Clint was stuck without a ride home until they left the bar.

Words and kisses made all my anger and jealousy from last night vanish. I should never have doubted him. He was too nice, and I told him so. I asked Clint if he joined in the Oak Park quest for female companionship.

"I told them I had a girl in Wilmette. They didn't push too hard on the subject, but they also said, 'So now you can have a girl in Oak Park as well.'"

That didn't surprise me in the least.

Tomorrow, Clint leaves with his parents for Paris. He said it was unfair to be heading to the city of love without the man he loves. *The man he loves*. He said it. *Those words*. I kept silent. Was it true or a way to defuse my anger? I could have said so much at that moment. Instead, I remained silent.

He promised to write me.

Postcards.

Being quiet any longer would be rude, and I'm always aware of my manners. "There will be so much to see in the City of Light, you'll have a wonderful time." More an obligatory comment than anything. I was so saddened that he was leaving. For so long I'd stopped caring. Stopped feeling. Stopped living. I'd given up hope and resigned myself to nothing more. Then Clint came into my life and everything changed. Of course I was upset. I knew what life was like before him. This ten-day absence was only a taste of the larger absence to come. *To hell with feeling selfish.* Clint was the one thing in life that mattered, and he was going away. I had every right to feel this way.

He looked at me and smiled. He seemed to know everything I was thinking.

Clint said his parents were taking him so they could all have a wonderful time before he went into service. "Mother feels worse about my being drafted than I do. Or at least worse than I used to feel," he added with a squeeze of my hand. "Now going in the service is worse, since I'm leaving something behind."

He said his father was already referring to him as "a military man."

After work, we went out for a nice dinner. My treat. Steaks and potatoes and salads along with a cocktail or two. Afterward, we came back here. We didn't sleep all night. We may have dozed a bit, but we held each other and talked and made our passion last. At around five, Clint headed back to his room. He said he still had to shower and pack some things. He also wanted to get a quick workout in before his parents came by at eight.

I said last night was a good bit of exercise. He leaned over and kissed me. "It certainly was."

I didn't want to see him go, but knew he had to. He kissed me again and told me to sleep in. When I awoke, it was ten thirty. *Gone*. Clint's plane to Paris was already in the air. The ghost of his scent remained. I could still smell him on the sheets, on my lips.

I lit a cigarette. Ten days.

Saturday April 28

He's gone. And his absence makes it so hard to go back to before. *Impossible*. Before Clint was another lifetime. Before Clint, I hid myself in habits and found pleasure in distracting myself from life. All so hollow. So routine. I couldn't simply climb on to the hamster wheel again. Things had changed.

I'd changed.

Less ready to settle. Less milquetoast.

Work was steady. The guys in Housewares and Appliances teased me about my boyfriend being out of town. Ella cackled along with them. Some adults never stray too far from the playground of childhood, or imagine a world grander than the sandbox. Small lives. Dismal prospects. They travel in packs. Fear makes them vicious. They're jerks. Why should they even care about my life? They care because they have nothing else.

Enough!

I turned to them and asked if they all had fun when they went out last night. Then I asked after their wife and kids. Said they must be so proud.

That shut them up all right. Made them wonder what I knew or had been told. Even Ella grew silent. She must have gone parking with one of them.

Maybe I'll turn the tables. Become the aggressor. Take a fistful of sand and throw it right back at them. Maybe I'll ask about their wife and kids *every day*.

After work I came back to the Lawson. I stumbled across two men getting it on in the stairwell. Fevered, hungry—I knew that state. I'd lived there for years. Sex was a thrill, a divine distraction, a hunt. That excitement was so often followed by a hollowness. The sense of being alone that I felt afterward could be so acute. Still, every tryst was worth the aftermath.

Sometimes there was more. Some men had the potential. The bond and the chemistry was there with Max, but the timing was wrong. First him, then me. Maybe it just wasn't meant to be. In the end we'd become friends who sometimes help each other out. Even that has cooled in the past few weeks, especially since Clint.

I looked at the men in the stairwell. I could go back to that sort of behavior, but it would never be the same. I'd see it for what it was. *Excitement. Distraction. Release.* I'd known something more, something deeper. These things worry me, especially with nothing but time on my hands. Worse, knowing that in a month Clint will be leaving for Lord knows how long. For now, it is just ten days.

I can't believe I wrote that—

JUST ten days.

That is all a matter of perspective. Away from my beloved, ten days seems an eternity.

Relativity. A tip of the hat to you, Mr. Einstein.

Sunday April 29

Another day passed in the waiting game. Life suspended. In grade school, my teachers always said I used time and materials wisely, so I decided to make good on their observation. During Clint's absence, I am going to use the gym a bit more, eat better, and pick up some extra shifts at work. I read a piece in the newspaper about a man who supplemented his income by buying stocks. I might do that with the money from extra shifts. I'll make this a time for improvement.

Max and Frankie came by this evening. We played cards until midnight. They are green with envy over my beau and full of questions about Clint.

How big? How often? How old?

None of your business. None of your business. And twenty-two.

Frankie called Clint dreamy. Max said I was a lucky dog. Both wanted to know my secret.

Those two are cut-ups. Won six dollars. Supplementing my income already. Ha!

Monday April 30

Dreamt of Clint in my arms. Us looking up at the cracks on the ceiling and listening to the creaks, the comings and goings of fellow Lawson residents. *Bliss*. Lying there, being nothing more than together. There is nothing more. Being together is everything. The salty scent of him, his masculine musk, the touch of his skin, the scratch of his dark morning beard, the weight of his body on mine. His smile, the ripple of muscles across his back when he moves to put on or take off his shirt. The way a shirt hangs at his hairy buttocks, like a curtain on the rise. The way his smile begins with a crinkling at his eyes that travels to his mouth. His lips. Those lips. Full. Inviting. The way I feel every time I see him. That rush that goes from head to crotch to heart all at the same time… a longing that fills my entire being. The ache without pain. No detail of Clint is too minor for appreciation. The all of him and the entirety of my desire seems to be in every bit of him.

Went to the movies after work today and saw *Breakfast at Tiffany's* for the third time. Enjoyable. Though I'm not a huge fan, Audrey Hepburn has never been more charming and George Peppard is beyond dreamy. Reminds me of a blond Clint in a way. *Tiffany's* is such an enjoyable film, but this time, I had other things in mind. Certain needs to be fulfilled. This time when I went to see it, I sat in the balcony. I was hungry and unafraid to partake in the shadowy activity. A stranger took me in his mouth. He was skilled and voracious. I closed my eyes and imagined Clint. I may have even called out his name. I know I did in my mind. I may not be faithful, but I am always loyal.

After gripping the armrests and releasing into that warm mouth, I was overcome with guilt, regret. I fled the balcony and was out on the street in under two minutes. Boy, but the cool air felt good. I walked back here instead of taking the bus. The moon was huge. So luminous the world seemed haunted, filled with the presence of something now gone. *Like me*.

I came back here to Chicago and North Dearborn. *Alone*.

That's what the balcony experience was about. Not sex, just a few minutes of not feeling so alone. In that respect, it failed miserably. Afterward, I felt more alone than ever. I pillow-hugged myself into a restless sleep.

Tuesday May 1

Strange dream. Much of it is vague with the morning light. In it, I remember Clint and me in his room, dozing on his bed. We heard something outside and opened the door. Instead of the tenth floor, we were suddenly much higher. Floor 24 was written on the door. Rolling hills and a meadow spread out before us. I took his hand in mine. As we looked out from our aerie, trees and flowers began to bud and bloom and spew clouds of pollen into the air. We could see it all happening, that dance of life, like a great gasp or expulsion from the plant world. The sun faded in the haze as the leaves on the trees matured and colored and fell. When I turned to Clint, he was no longer standing beside me. The hand I was holding was Max's. When I looked again the hand I was holding was my own. I awoke disoriented. That happens very rarely. Usually I don't dream.

Today, I was irritable at work and in no mood for any coworker comments or shenanigans. Every customer seemed either a pest or a drain or both. Allergies only contributed to my testiness. A leftover from my foliage dream? Ha! Everything is in bloom. Lovely to look at, but it gives me a headache right behind my eyes. The explosions of pollen make breathing difficult. Usually my allergies only last a couple of weeks. Boy, but it is painful while it's happening, but then I forget all about the pain until next year. Maybe now that I've written it down and committed that discomfort to paper, I'll remember.

I went to the TV room and watched *American Bandstand*. I have no idea why. Maybe to feel more connected to younger people. Clint? So much jumping around. The dances are all unfamiliar—the twist, the jerk, the mashed potato, the Watusi. Not the best choice of program when you're experiencing a headache. I fled after fifteen minutes. Back to my room and reread *Giovanni's Room* by James Baldwin. Still my favorite book. I reread it every year, along with Gore Vidal's *The City and the Pillar*. Both authors have this wonderful ability to take you into the world of taboo male love. I need to keep the memory of that world fresh until Clint returns.

So happy to see that Marilyn is feeling better and making another movie, *Something's Got to Give* with Dean Martin and Cyd Charisse. I might be the only person I know who loved both *The Misfits* and *Let's Make Love*. She can do no wrong.

Wednesday May 2

Today, I was called into the office for wearing a wrinkled shirt. There is so much humbling involved in growing older. I wouldn't have thought twice about this sort of thing at twenty or twenty-five. I would be able to see the censure for what it was. But at forty-two, an attire warning has such an air of shame—the lecture by the floor manager and signing the employee warning form. Knowing that degrading slip of paper is now tucked into my file and will be dredged into view during my employee review. The inevitable promise to iron or have items dry cleaned. This has more to do with power than a wrinkled shirt.

I planned to wake up early and iron. The task was on my list. Instead, I woke up and thought about Clint. *Longed for. Ached for. Fantasized about…* and forgot the time. Maybe I should have said my shirt is wrinkled because I was masturbating. Ha! That would have fixed them. My intentions were good, and then it was suddenly time to leave with no time to iron. The cards are stacked. Men with a family have a ready enough excuse: "Sorry I'm late, the baby was up all night." "Sorry my suit is wrinkled, my wife didn't get the dry cleaning picked up." The acceptable combinations are endless. As a bachelor, I am seen as having nothing better to do with my time than iron or be on call or stay late or any number of things. As a bachelor, it is presumed that my work is my mate. I'm forty-two and without a family, so it's assumed I have no personal life.

Anger from the censure remained with me throughout the day. *Bastards!* I wish I had the nerve to speak my mind. The end of my shift could not come soon enough. I went to the movies again tonight. Again, I sat in the balcony. The movies are an escape, and carrying on in the balcony was an even greater escape. I desperately needed to escape the facts of life. The darkened balcony was another world. We seem to appear as the eyes adjust, an entire community of men emerging from the shadows and finding a bit of solace in lush antiquated surroundings. Fitting, I suppose. This time, I didn't leave after I ejaculated. This time I stayed and watched and participated some more. I had nothing and no one waiting for me at the Lawson, only more of this. As I caroused, I snickered to think, *If only my floor manager knew*. The secrecy of all this filled me with power. *If they only knew*. There is so much more to my life than working five days a week at M_____.

Back to the Lawson, I checked my mail and found a postcard from Clint. A colorized montage of Paris landmarks on the front and on the back. "Paris is lovely. A large city that is, at the same time, intimate. Gorgeous weather. Taking plenty of pictures. Mom shops and hits the museums. Father took a meeting and can't stop working even here. Thinking of you, Clint."

Of course I felt guilty for my behavior in the theater, but for what it's worth, I was thinking of him too. Or at least the lack of him.

Went to the TV room and watched *The Dick Van Dyke Show* with Max and Frankie and a few other guys. Watched about half of *Naked City* after that. By 9:30, I was exhausted. Ironed when I got back to my room.

Thursday May 3

Clint called early this morning. The hall phone rang, and then I heard a knock on my door. Frankie said the call was for me. Actually he said I had a "gentleman caller," which was rather clever. Frankie always figures the campiest way to say things. Luckily, I was still home. I'd intended to leave for work early and grab a breakfast plate along the way. Instead, I polished my shoes.

Wow! My heart sure skipped a beat to hear Clint's voice on the line. I asked if everything was okay. He said he'd explain later. Transatlantic calls were very expensive. Clint said he was coming home early. When I asked why, he only said there was a change of plans. He started to say something more when the operator cut in and asked for additional francs. Clint said he'd see me on Sunday and fill me in on the details then. Our conversation lasted less than thirty seconds. Sunday! He'll be back on Sunday! Three days until his return. I wonder what happened. Nothing bad I hope, though secretly, I don't care. As long as he comes home. I walked back from the phone with a spring in my step.

Frankie was in his doorway. "Good news I take it?"
I nodded.

"Lucky man," was all Frankie said. He was right. I was lucky. My prayers had been answered. I whistled all the way to work. Even allergies weren't going to get me down.

Friday May 4

Relentless rain. I brought an umbrella and took the bus, and still my shoes were soaked by the time I got to work. Never felt as though I got dry all day. The weather kept the customers away. A very long eight hours.

I really need to do something career-wise other than working at M_____. I've been standing and staring from behind this counter at this dead-end job for over a decade now. This place is comfortable. Easy. This is a job I fell into and never had the wherewithal to climb out of. The only real challenge in this place is to maintain my sanity. At M_____, I know what to expect and what is expected of me. Certainty and routine can numb a person to so much of life. Clint changed all that. He roused me from sleep and made me feel what it's like to be alive. To thrill at the unexpected. Being with Clint makes me see how sad my "career" is. Shouldn't I get some level of excitement or satisfaction from what I do? Maybe I'm expecting too much for a paycheck, or maybe I'm expecting too little from myself.

Don't know where all this is coming from. Nothing is wrong. Nothing is different. Nothing unusual. Maybe this is just what it's like to see the world through younger eyes. Suddenly I've been roused and look up to wonder what happened. Where did all my promise and ambition go? Who is that guy in the mirror?

Boy, but I am on a jag. Probably coming about because Clint is coming home. I can't help but wonder why the Paris vacation was cut short. Two more days, and I'll know. Two more days, and we'll be together.

Tonight, I went down to the gym for a steam. I always sleep better after a good sweat. Max was there. We chatted a bit. That silver-haired devil is still so handsome. Debonaire. We have shared a bed and socialized, but at the same time, I know so little about his life. When I saw Max this evening, I asked if he had plans for the weekend. He told me no. Max seemed down so I asked if everything was okay. He shrugged, "My son's birthday is this weekend."

I had no idea.

When I asked if he was going to see him, Max said no and leaned closer. He said he used to have a wife and son. "Technically, I still do." he laughed, "I worked as a history teacher out in the suburbs. I loved my job. Loved teaching…" Through the hiss of steam, Max explained that last summer he was caught in a bathhouse raid in Lincoln Park. The authorities saw fit to print his name, home address, and employer in the newspaper. "The only person who was more upset than the school board was my wife." Max said his wife divorced him. He lost his job. He moved in here. Before today, I didn't know any of this. Before today, I didn't know his story. We all have our secrets. Before today, all I knew about Max was that we connected and that I liked him. He was fun and attractive and worked as a waiter at the Silver Chalice Supper Club.

"Everything was taken from me," he added.

Max made me promise to be careful. "Some people think nothing of ruining other people's lives. Some folks even relish it." He added that he was fortunate. "After all, I'm still here." Max told me to keep his business under my hat. "I don't like people knowing my life, but I wanted to tell you. Frankie knows too." Max slapped his hands to his thighs and said that was all in the past. I assured him I wouldn't breathe a word. Poor Max. He's a good man. We all have to stick together in this underground.

I told Max a bit more about Clint. What I was feeling about him. That he told me he loved me. Max wished me well. I hadn't opened up to anyone about those sorts of things. I really had no one to confide in usually. The situation with Max had simply presented itself and Max was always easy to talk to. It felt good to share some things, though I'm still not comfortable with specifics. Maybe moderation is the key in disclosure. If you trust no one, you'll end up with no one to trust.

"Don't let something like that slip through your fingers," Max said as he exited the steam room. "Love is worth fighting for."

Saturday May 5

One more day. Twenty-four hours until Clint is home and in my arms. I was going to write "just twenty-four hours," but I know how long a day can be when anticipation is so strong. Everything seems on hold until we're together again. All is a matter of waiting and wading through the mundane. I requested Monday and Tuesday off.

At work, we had a pre-opening staff meeting on the recent rise in the improper filling out of sales receipts—putting the wrong date, forgetting to add item stock number, etc. If I ever needed a reason to reevaluate the work portion of my life, it was that meeting. Talk about mundane! Sometimes I think management must concoct these things simply to give their job meaning. Everything seems even more insignificant in light of Clint's coming home. That makes me wonder what will happen when he eventually goes into the service. Will my entire world be on hold for those two or three years? Women endured it all through WWI and WWII and Korea, so I don't know why I think I am so special. Maybe just because it's me. Maybe because my separation can never be common knowledge.

Sunday May 6

Today.
The day is finally here.
Not sure when, only that Clint is coming home today.

This morning, I heard a knock on my door. It was
him. He pushed me inside and back upon the bed. He
was so aggressive and excited to see me. To be with me.
I quite loved it. *Ravenous*. He had me twice without
stopping. Twenty-two is a great thing. Afterward, his
arm around me, smiles upon our faces, and a cigarette for
me. Head on his chest, I could hear his heartbeat. The
moment was everything. There was no world outside this
room. I was sure if we opened the door, we would see
only desolation, or maybe outer space. How could
anything exist outside of this?

I asked about his return. He said he'd tell me soon. I
write these words while he is getting us sandwiches and
a bottle of wine. I wanted to come along, but he insisted.
"We're going to have a picnic," he said, buckling his
pants and heading out the door. Clint promised to explain
everything when he returned. The mystery of it all had
my imagination running wild, only now explanations
seem secondary. All that matters is that he's home, and
we're together again.

Monday May 7

Apparently, Clint's mother guessed what was going on. She noticed how her son was behaving in Paris, his distraction, his longing. The first and second night when she asked him what was bothering him, he said it was *Nothing*. On the third night, he began to cry. He said he was in love and had to leave for the Army soon, and he was separated from the man he loved. Clint said his mother might not have understood everything he was saying, but she knew love. And she loved him. She booked their return at once. She said it was more important that he was home with his beloved than abroad without him.

I said his mother must be very open-minded. Clint said she loved him very much and that love trumped all else. When I said she sounded extraordinary, Clint added that she blamed herself for his turning out queer. When I asked Clint why, he shrugged and said it was just something she'd read in a magazine. He said that was the way his mother learned everything.

"She suspected you were my boyfriend, the man she and my father had met when they came to the Lawson." Clint said his mother made up an excuse to his father about coming home. "He was taking meetings and working anyway. For my father, it never was a family vacation." Clint said his father would send him into the Army for sure if he knew about all this. "He'd send me into the Army, or to a priest, or a psychologist, and if all else failed, he'd probably have me institutionalized. He's a conservative Army man, and I've heard him say things of that sort," admitted Clint. "A son like me would destroy his legacy and bring him great shame. He wouldn't see this as something I am, but as something I'm doing to him. Everything is about him. His ego is enormous."

I wasn't keen on getting to know his father.

Clint took my hand. He said he needed to confess something. Before, when he disappeared for a few days and said he went home, he'd actually gone in for his physical. He said May 28 is when he is expected to appear for boot camp. His last day of work is the 25th, and he is leaving for a weekend with his parents on the 26th. That was the concession he had to make to come home early from Paris. His mother was planning an elaborate send-off party for her boy. One last weekend with her son was all she asked. Clint said he couldn't disappoint her.

I didn't want to be disappointed either, but I can't think about that now. The thought of being apart again is nothing I want to dwell upon. That sort of thing is pointless. I have to focus on the time we have.

Tuesday May 8

Yesterday was perfect, except for Clint's disclosure about our remaining time together. I mentioned the option of dishonorable discharge again but boy, Clint sure put his foot down. He refused to even consider it. I said he had done nothing dishonorable. He wouldn't be lying. Telling the truth was all it would take for us to be together. He said that sort of truth was impossible. I was pained to realize that, to Clint, some things were bigger than our togetherness.

"The truth would kill my father. To his way of thinking, I might as well be a Soviet. I want him to be proud of me. I've wanted that since I was a kid." Clint said it so directly that I felt for him. I didn't have the heart to tell him that he shouldn't have to earn his father's love. I spoke from experience. That was a lesson I learned the hard way.

Clint's tone abruptly changed. He said something along the lines of, *It feels right to serve my country*. That was as false as I had ever heard him sound. I didn't hold it against him. Clint was scared and desperate to convince himself. Our exchange was tense and as close as we've come to a fight. Clint reddened and said he had things to do. I didn't see him again until after dinner.

Around seven, he knocked on my door. He sheepishly apologized for earlier and said he didn't want to discuss the subject. He said it was easier for him to accept his lot if he considered his Army service as inevitable and the right thing to do. I need to respect that.

I apologized for lecturing and said it was none of my affair.

He moved closer and held me in his arms. "I'd consider you an interested party… or maybe you're not interested." Two minutes later, we were naked and back on the bed. We'd returned to our idyllic place, a paradise unmoored to any reality except the one we created together. Our lovemaking was fevered, rough, and then gentle. When he came inside of me, he whispered in my ear that he loved me. He'd never said those words during, not like that, and the sound of it made my eyes mist. I lifted my head and kissed him. "Always," I replied, looking deep into his eyes.

"Always what?"

"I'll always love you."

Clint smiled. Content. I understood his wanting, maybe even needing, to hear those words. Especially in the light of pending armed service.

When I awakened an hour or so later, Clint was still asleep. We were lying face to face. I dreaded a return to work in the morning and the recurrence of the mundane. Clint still had two more days free.

Thursday May 10

How could I be so careless! I left my journal in my briefcase. I was going to write in it during lunch, but I got distracted. I put my briefcase in my locker in the morning and ended up going to Woolworth's during break and eating at the lunch counter. At five, I was so eager to be with Clint that I forgot the briefcase entirely. By the time I realized what had happened, it was too late to go back to M_____.

The contents of this journal could have me arrested, fired, ostracized, unemployed, and condemned. Sure, the sodomy laws may have been repealed on January 1 this year. And I was both pleased and surprised that Illinois was the first state in the country to do so. But people's minds don't change quite so easily. I know how the police can be with the law and homosexuals. A lot of policeman probably don't care that the law has changed. Legislation doesn't add up to a hill of beans to those fellows. Most still call us perverts. Men can be arrested for all sorts of things. Employers can still fire you and landlords can still turn you away. The newspaper would love to print a juicy bit like this along with my real name and address as well as Clint's. Even Max is mentioned in these pages, and Max has already lost his job, his wife, and his son. His wasn't the first story like that I've heard. Some of the those tales end in suicide, others with imprisonment or institutionalization.

Frankie is mentioned in those pages as well… and others too.

The Lawson already had a whispered reputation. The fact of Clint and Max and Frankie and myself living here would only give my journal credence, additional gravitas. Everyone seems to know "a person whose cousin had stayed here once and…"

Unspeakable doings.

Unnatural goings-on.

A modern day Sodom and Gomorrah.

Blah. Blah.

Perhaps I have a reputation as well. Maybe the contents of this journal won't surprise a lot of people but merely offer proof and a justification for their disgust. The difference in response is that of a giggle versus a sneer. With a giggle, there are no details. With the sneer, all is known… or enough to imagine. *That pervert had sexual relations in the theater balcony and in a public steam room and in a public restroom and at the YMCA.* I can only imagine the disgust. Just being a homosexual is a threat to manhood and womanhood and families and the American Way of Life. Insidious. Undermining. Many see us as worse than communists.

I, Joseph M_____, hereby declare everything in this journal to be an experimental work of fiction.

Stating that will be enough to get me off the hook, but I could never swear in a court of law that none of this was real. I could never renounce the past few weeks. Only since Clint came into my life have I been truly alive. All that led up to Clint was mostly sleepwalking, a preparation before getting down to the real business of living. Before Clint, I felt I was playing an ongoing game that wasn't terribly engaging. Now, after playing the game for so long, I've finally won. The reward is well worth the effort. How can anything in my past have been wrong when it brought me to Clint? With Clint, the meandering and seemingly pointless path of life finally makes sense. But this game has a twist. The prize vanishes at the end. The paradise is a mirage. Such crap. I've given up too easily for too many years. It's time I started believing in happy endings.

After dinner and a nap, my mood changed for the better. I went to the TV room to watch *Dr. Kildare*. Clint headed to the gym.

With Clint back from Paris, I'm back to being drunk with love, intoxicated by it. I'm sleep-deprived and dreamy. Euphoric sounds melodramatic, but there have been so many times recently when I feel as though heaven has actually arrived. I cannot fathom that what I'm living now and what I'd been living before I met Clint, are both called life. We can have two dozen kinds of cheeses, but we only have one word for life. That common experience that we all share differs more than anything else on the planet.

Clint returns to work tomorrow. Time is passing too quickly. The thought of this ending or being put on hold, the thought of Clint going into the Army, takes my breath away and leaves an ache inside. I'm no fool. I've lived enough to realize the futility of worrying about the future. I know enough to make the most of what I have, but knowing doesn't necessarily change the way a person feels.

Friday May 11

My paranoia seems unfounded. If someone had taken my briefcase from my locker and read my journal, I doubt they would have returned it. Besides, I would've heard something by now. Boy, was I fortunate! Didn't say a word about the scare to Clint. No use giving him an additional worry. Clint doesn't even know this journal exists. Ha! These pages are like having an unknown intimate. A confessor and a confidante. Clint is still too young to see the importance of writing things down. Preserving moments. Capturing time. He still sees through the eyes of youth and thinks things will last forever. Experience has taught me differently. Life can be so lonely without memories, and sometimes even with them. This journal is a risk, but it provides something precious, something worth the worry.

We lunched in the park today. Wonderful sunshine and a refreshing breeze off Lake Michigan. Every winter, I grow to hate Chicago. By March, I vow to move to a milder climate. Then, by the end of April, I fall in love with the Windy City all over again. When she is in bloom, no place is better.

Clint and I bought ice-cream cones and walked along the shore. We didn't speak much at all. Words seemed unnecessary, even intrusive. Being with one another was conversation enough. We were late returning from lunch. The floor manager wrote me up. I've been here over a decade, and this second infraction of "fifteen minutes tardy" is cause for alarm. Middle management grows very threatened when rules are ignored. They have nothing else. They are little more than the custodians of a tight ship. If I'd never met Clint, I may well have aged into some sad creature like Mr. S_____. His position is for those workers who give their all for the company but have no leadership capabilities. As he wrote me up for the second time in a month, I actually stood there feeling sorry for him. *Thank goodness Clint saved me from this fate,* I thought as Mr. S _____ added another colored slip of paper to my file.

Ella will have a field day with this.

After work, Clint and I mock-celebrated my being written up by ducking into a tiki bar for a cocktail or two. Clint told me his mother called him at work and asked how things were going. Since Clint's parents are friends with the owner, the rules are bent. Late from lunch and a personal phone call. The rest of us would be on very thin ice, but Mr. S_____ would never dare write up Clint.

When Clint's mother asked how things were going, she meant how were things going with me. When Clint told me that, I could not believe it. When I said she must be one in a million, Clint said she loved him and wanted to see him happy. I told Clint she must be one of the most open-minded people in Illinois. I asked him if he realized how lucky he was. He said he did.

My mother died when I was young, so I've no idea how she would've responded. I remember her smell. I remember her telling me my fingerprints mirrored the wind patterns on the night I was born. Untrue, of course, but a lovely notion nonetheless. I still meet up once in a while with my brother and his wife. They know about me, but pretend that they don't. They tolerate me in spite of what I am. My father is a different story. He disowned me. After he found out, he gave me eight hours to get out. He said he wasn't going to be the laughingstock of the neighborhood. I saw my father once downtown, but I don't think he saw me. That was two years ago, and it was the first time I'd seen him in a decade. He looked much older. I don't even know if he'd recognize me. I stopped caring years ago. That's not true. I haven't stopped caring. Indifference is impossible. More accurate to say I've developed a thick skin about the issue. I abandoned any expectation of a reconciliation years ago.

The evening was so clear and lovely, Clint and I went up to the roof and lay on the tarpaper and looked up at the sky. The city light washed many of the stars from the nighttime sky, but several constellations were still visible—the Big Dipper, Orion. Light from hundreds of years ago was coming from those distant stars to shine down upon us tonight. A magical thought. In that moment, the world and everything in it seemed an orchestrated slice of perfection and we were part of the symphony. We kissed a bit before we heard the rooftop door open. No cause for alarm. Others taking advantage of the night. We heard laughter against the buzz of the neon YMCA sign. The interlopers were another pair of lovers eager to share the starshine. I whispered to Clint that we should go back to the room. When we passed the two guys on the way to the door, I smiled. They nodded our direction, and we nodded back. We were acknowledging more than simply one another. We were acknowledging the situation. That small sharing felt so good. Comrades in the underground. Small moments such as these vanish without a journal.

Saturday May 12

Though I have tried to avoid the inevitable, only two weeks remain until we say good-bye, two weeks until Clint returns to his parents' house in Wilmette for his farewell visit before heading off to basic training. He mentioned his father and grandfather were both career military men. When he flunked out of school for engineering, it was decided that he would carry on the tradition. *Not he decided, but it was decided.* His future is a group decision, and he doesn't seem part of the group. I know I'll be courting an argument, but I want to tell Clint how poisonous it is to have his life path decided for him. The trappings of wealth and status and the expectations of class have never seemed clearer. Suddenly getting kicked out of the house doesn't seem so bad in comparison.

When I think about the future, I want to say, "What about me?" I want to ask Clint if that means that, come May 25th, everything is over between us. Is this all going to become a memory? A few journal pages? Is what we have simply a matter of getting something out of his system before he settles down with some nice girl from a good Protestant family? Will my existence become just a dirty little secret that Clint and his mother will take to their graves? Or maybe things will continue. Clint will have his wife and his ideal life, and I'll be the indiscretion he keeps on the side. I want to talk to him about it, but I don't want to upset him.

We both worked at the store today but agreed to go on separate lunches. Clint went for Greek food with Nick from Housewares and Appliances. They were laughing when they returned. Was Clint that good of an actor? The sound of their shared jokes irritated me. I did not want to share Clint with anyone, especially Nick. He asked Clint to go bowling with the guys that night. Clint agreed. I was furious when he told me. Should I have to remind him that we have so little time? So little, and yet that is what he chose to do. I wanted to ask what he was thinking. I shouldn't have to say anything. I had my pride. I said nothing. Instead, I saw *The Premature Burial* starring Ray Milland and sat in the balcony. I could relate to the fear of being buried alive. I knew the Poe story, but I don't recall too much about the movie. I was distracted by the goings-on and eventually engaged in them. If Clint wasn't going to take this seriously, I wasn't either. I have to protect myself. I am the one he'll be leaving, maybe forever. I need to try to make us mean less to me. But I don't know if that is possible.

When I got home, Clint was talking to Frankie and waiting outside my room. When he saw me approach, Frankie winked and headed for the elevators, adding, "Don't do anything I wouldn't do." He is so cheeky! He was off to tend bar.

Clint said he'd ducked out of bowling early to come and be with me. I said I thought he'd be late so I went to the movies. I told him I had a sinus headache and needed to get to sleep. I had to make some excuse. If Clint wanted to make love, he would know I was already spent. He kissed me good night and went to his room. I hope he couldn't taste the indiscretion on my lips. I feel like an old fool and a heel, a stupid and impulsive heel.

Sunday May 13

From a retail perspective, Sunday browsing is a welcome relief from the frenzy most Saturdays bring. M_____ is having a respectable spring. They give bonuses when we break records. Fingers crossed. Selling more dark, thin ties than usual. Plain colors or stripes. Patterns and such seem to be collecting dust. I was thinking of buying one for Clint today as a surprise, but I reconsidered. So unromantic to buy someone a tie when you work at a tie and umbrella counter. I do want to buy him something to remember me by after he goes in the military, but not that. Maybe a money clip or a wristwatch with a vague inscription, something like *Always* and then my initials. The thought of buying him something like that terrifies me. It's an acknowledgement that he is really leaving, and this magical spring, like every spring, is going to end.

I wonder how much appeal being with me will hold after he has been in the service and lived a bit more. I don't want to be remembered as the old flame who gave him the money clip or the watch. *A stuffy gift from a sad older man he knew a long time ago.* I don't want to be a memory. I want to be the man he dreams of, longs for, and eventually comes home to… but I'm no fool. I know the world we live in. Many would like to see our kind destroyed or altered. Even those who are tolerant don't want to see us happy. We're not quite *that* deserving. We're a statistic, a sad reality of modern society. Being capable of happiness would make us a bit too human.

I'm being dramatic. I must still be tired from work.

Clint had the day off. We made love this morning, a terrific way to plaster a smile on my face for hours. Afterward, I had to bound from bed and shower and dash. My big burly man looked so good lying on my bed as I kissed him to leave. Furry and content. Arms behind his head smiling. That hairy chest. Those muscled biceps. Dimples. A gleam in his eye. I kissed him again. I wanted to rip that sheet from him and join him for another round. No.

I breezed through the employee entrance of M_____ wearing a contented smile. Loving Clint keeps me sane. Love allows me to see what is important and still smile at all the things that aren't. That's a priceless perspective to have, especially when you work a retail counter. I'm not seeing the world through rose-colored glasses; I am discovering that the world can, in fact, be rose colored.

After Clint leaves, I wonder if the color of my world will dull and fade and once again I'll be left with the drab grays of my former life. Will thoughts of Clint buoy my spirits enough to keep the colors and my outlook vibrant? I wonder if this journal will suffice. Will the memory of his eyes or his sleeping beside me be enough? Will the memory of his body, his smell, and his taste sustain me? Will I only see my life for what it's lacking? I haven't a crystal ball. I don't have any way of knowing. All I can say is whatever the cost, the joy of loving and being loved has been worth more than any price. This has been the highlight of my life. Nothing else comes close.

Monday May 14

Nothing is as wonderful as having a day off together. The world becomes our world, and the day becomes a canvas. We create what we want things to be, and it always seems to be a masterpiece. Today, we went to Lincoln Park and strolled along the lagoon up through the zoo and then the conservatory. A zoo can be a lonely place when you come by yourself. All you see are the cages and the bars. Being with Clint was like seeing it all through a new pair of eyes. He transforms everything we do because he transforms me. He has awakened my sense of wonder and awe. He has awakened me.

As we walked along the lagoon and threw crackers to the ducks, several swan boats floated by filled with, what I imagined to be, courting couples. I could tell Clint wanted to say something. Eventually, Clint looked out over the water and told me he was afraid. He said he didn't want to go to war. "I don't think I can kill, for my country or for any other reason."

I didn't know what to say. I may have said, "Be sure to tell them that," which is either brilliant or idiotic advice. His innate gentleness is endearing, especially given his muscular physique. I doubt the US Armed Forces will agree with me. They prize different abilities.

We walked along in silence for a bit. Then at the entrance to the zoo, he abruptly seemed to have put those worrisome thoughts behind him. He'd returned to the present. The previous moments seemed nothing more than a passing cloud.

At the Lincoln Park Zoo, we enjoyed the penguins and the seals the most. They were the only species that looked like they were having fun. Many of the other animals seemed to mostly be bored or pining for elsewhere.

The gardens outside the conservatory were spectacular—lush and colorful and aromatic. I loved it, but my allergies were acting up. A small price to pay. Minuscule given the rewards. Inside the conservatory was a dream world. As we walked the path through the towering greenery, I imagined us walking through a strange, wild, and timeless new world we had created. Like the Lawson on West Chicago Ave., 1962 was merely another home address. Our world was outside of time and place. Maybe Clint and I were residences as well, and our bodies merely another form of address for some greater cosmic love. Perhaps our forms were only vessels for a more enduring spirit. Maybe we're only vessels for Love. *Listen to me!* The bliss of it all fills me with lunatic notions. Being with Clint makes me feel brilliant and moronic, foolish and wise, caring and detached all at once.

We made love when we came back to the Lawson. We were silent and focused, with no boundaries between our bodies, between us. *Fluid. One. A single organism. He inside me. Me enveloping him.* We were at the point where giving and receiving pleasure overlap to become something more. We were another manifestation of Love.

Before Clint crept back to his own room in the middle of the night, he kissed me on the forehead and whispered to have a good day. Clint has Tuesday off. His mother is coming into town. They're having lunch.

Tuesday May 15

Work went smoothly. Had my display cases complimented by Mr. M_____ himself. Boy but the floor manager had nothing but smiles for me after that, and even those jerks in Housewares and Appliances were sure quiet. Mr. M_____ never complimented the workers directly. At least, not before today. Sometimes a manager would give us a note that said something like "Tuck Shirt" or "Haircut!" When he communicated with us, it was typically to correct behavior. Someone had recently received a note that said, "You don't look like you enjoy being here. Remember that at your next job." Attached to the note was their pink slip. Mr. M_____ had not built his empire by being a pushover.

As I was leaving work, there was a folk singer on the corner. I went and listened to her, and a moment later, a yellow taxi pulled up. Clint was inside and seated beside him was a middle-aged woman I recognized as his mother. She leaned over Clint and introduced herself as Constance. I shook her hand and said it was nice to see her again. Clint looked from one of us to the other and just grinned.

"We're taking you to dinner," said Constance, "No ifs, ands, or buts!" They'd had quite a day today. The cab's trunk was filled with shopping bags. Constance said she needed new things after her weight loss the past winter. Her doctor had prescribed her some diet pills. She'd lost seventeen pounds since the first of January. She said it was the first resolution she had ever kept. She talked endlessly. The taxi took us to a wonderful steakhouse on Wells Street in Old Town.

The interior of the restaurant was dark. The waitress showed us to a booth. Constance ordered a scotch. Clint and I ordered beers. More small talk ensued, quite a bit of small talk that saw us through another round of drinks, through the placing of our food order, and throughout the meal. The weather. Shopping downtown. Working at M_____. We talked about everything except Clint and I or Clint and the Army. I wasn't sure if the topics were taboo, or Constance was just too nervous to broach either subject. I certainly wasn't going to bring either thing up.

After dinner, Clint excused himself to go the men's room. Smiling as she watched him go, Constance lit a cigarette and asked me if I loved her son. I was shocked and eventually uttered yes. She shook her head. I could tell she'd had one cocktail too many. Constance said if I really loved Clint, this conversation wouldn't be taking place. "If you loved Clint and wanted the best for him, his happiness would mean everything to you. Joseph, you know what he could expect by staying with you, by living that kind of life."

I didn't know what to say. I thought she wanted Clint to be happy. I made her son happy.

Constance said she had a good idea what he could expect from a life like that and from a future with the likes of me. She said she had let him come home early from Paris and spend his last few weeks at the Lawson. What more did I want? I wanted to tell her I wanted a lot more, but I was too shocked by her behavior to respond. Besides, forever was not a word she wanted to hear, and

Constance was clearly a woman who was used to hearing what she wanted to hear.

She told me the time was right to break things off with Clint. "Now. Before he goes into the service. Then this will all seem like a puerile phase to him. Once he's in the Army, this will all seem a lifetime ago."

I was speechless and still at a loss for something to say when Clint returned from the lavatory. He asked what we'd been discussing. Constance said we'd just been getting to know one another and having a little chat. She picked up the tab. Her cab dropped us off at the Lawson before taking her to the train station. "I've got to be on the eight forty-five." She hugged Clint and kissed me on the cheek. *A Judas kiss*. Did she have any idea what she was asking me to do? She was asking me to abandon the only thing than meant something in my life.

Clearly it isn't Clint's happiness she cares about, but her own.

I didn't say a word to Clint. How could I? Evidently, he saw his mother as something much different than what she was, at least what she was to those who threatened her way of life. Or the way she preferred things to be. Telling him the truth might make him hate me. Stuck between a rock and a hard place.

Clint and I climbed into bed, and I held him in my arms. We were both so quiet. I didn't know what to say. I was still in shock over Constance's audacity.

Clint said he was glad I liked his mother.

When I eventually spoke, I told him about Mr. M_____ complimenting my display case. Clint was already asleep.

Wednesday May 16

We walked to work this morning. Clint asked me why I was so quiet. I said I was just sleepy, "or maybe it's my allergies." I mentioned every possibility I could think of except the truth. He asked me again what I thought of his mother. I said she was chic and very nice. He said she liked me, too. Clint said he could tell. Who knows? Under different circumstances, she may have liked me. As it was, even if she spoke to me out of love for her son, I loathed her for putting me in this position. I doubted she cared about Clint, not really. I suspected it was more accurate to say she cared about HER son. One was a person and one was a possession.

And while we're on the subject of loathing, I realize I'm irritable, but is there any reason that *American Bandstand* has to be on TV every night of the week? Dick Clark has to be the most overexposed man in the country right now. *Enough!*

Thursday May 17

This secret is insidious. The conversation I had with Constance is infecting all the time Clint and I spent together. Perhaps Constance knew it would. Maybe she is more cunning and calculating than I supposed. I can't let all this unpleasantness taint the magic of our love. So often making a sacrifice and being a martyr is praised, but oftentimes, it is just plain stupid. I'd sacrificed so much in my life because I didn't see myself as worthy. That was then. Something had changed in me. I wasn't stepping aside. Not this time.

I could no longer remain silent. Fortified by a couple cocktails, I told Clint everything Constance had said. Clint paused for a moment and shook his head. He said he wondered if something like that had happened. He said she loved him but probably felt like she was losing him on all fronts, to the Army and now to me as well. "She does not like being denied things. The Army is out of her control, but you are not."

I asked Clint how he got to be so smart about people, and he pointed to his ears. "I listen," he said softly. Clint said it was the key to understanding everyone.

I asked him what was the key to understanding me. Clint smiled and leaned over and kissed me. Beckoning. "It's not your ears." He kissed farther down. "Or your chest." Kissing farther. "Or your stomach." He unzipped my pants and took me in his mouth. Bingo! In moments, we were both naked. He was almost brutal. A hairy beast. But I liked being taken by him.

Ravaged. Used. Slapped. Abused. Primal. Pure.

A short time later, we were lying spent and sweating in one another's arms. After a few moments of silence, I lifted my head from Clint's chest and asked him not to say I'd said anything about the talk with his mother. I didn't want to be the cause of any family trouble or discord. He said not to worry. He didn't like family discord either, but he did mention later that the issue needed to be addressed. "She needs to be clear about a few things, namely us."

Hearing those words, I questioned what I had done. I wondered if I should have kept my mouth shut.

Friday May 18

I saw Max down in the lobby this morning getting his mail. He looked like a prize fighter after a losing bout. He was sporting a black eye and had a wide bandage across the bridge of his nose. He pulled me aside and said he was walking the retaining wall along Oak Street Beach. Max liked to go cruising there. *Trade*. A cute guy in chinos gave him the sign and then ducked into the underpass. "When I followed, they jumped me. A couple guys. Calling me the most horrible names. Calling me scum. Unnatural. Pervert. Sodomite. Lefty. Pansy. They robbed me and said I had it coming."

I asked Max what he was going to do. Max said he couldn't report it to the police. "They would want to know why I was down there. Where was I going? What was I up to? They would look up my history and see the raid. Then I'd become the criminal. Cops do it all the time. That's the way things work in Daley's Chicago." Max was right. I didn't know what to say to him. Sometimes being brutalized just seemed the price we pay. Poor man. He couldn't catch a break. When he walked away, I could see he was limping.

Clint confronted his mother. I should have seen that coming. I asked him not to, but he did anyway. He asked her how she could say something like that to me. She said she expected as much and added that I was against her. *He wants you all to himself*. Me! As though my telling Clint about our conversation was the problem.

Constance probably hates me even more than before. Now she must think me a sniveling snitch as well as someone unwilling to play her game. Clint said she called me a clerk. She supposedly said, "I can't believe this is all happening because of some *clerk*."

She said she wanted him home. He said she worked herself into a rage. Clint said she could be bad. Unreasonable. "But these new diet pills were making her worse. *A monster*."

Constance spoke to her friend at M_____ and had Clint's position terminated immediately. As of *now*. His time card was gone when he came back from lunch. Constance said if he didn't come home, there would be trouble. *Plenty of trouble*. She said she'd tell Clint's father all about what had been going on.

Clint said he knew it was no idle threat and shuddered at the thought. His father didn't get mad, his father took action. Swift and devastating action. He said his father would make big trouble. "He knows people. He knows how to ruin lives. He is involved in some of the more shadowy areas of the military and intelligence." When he saw the look of disbelief in my eyes, he added, "No really. This isn't just cloak-and-dagger talk. He has connections, lots of them."

Clint said he needed to get back to Wilmette tonight. "I can't let her tell my father." I told Clint I wasn't afraid. *I lied*. The thought of someone powerful actively working to destroy my modest life was terrifying. My world was fragile and built upon secrets. My liberty was dependent on going unnoticed. This would change all that. I remembered the devastating sweep of the McCarthy Senate hearings quite well. Those were powerful people. Artists. Writers. Intellectuals. They were connected. I was none of those things. Living in the shadows makes a person extremely vulnerable. Sometimes we die from exposure. However, sometimes in life you're faced with heroic decisions and you have to decide what is and isn't worth fighting for. This was my time. My battle. And Clint was worth the fight.

I made him promise not to go back home to Wilmette. I didn't trust his mother. I told him it was a trick. I said, "They will keep you there. We can't let them separate us. We have to stick together."

Eventually he saw my logic and agreed. I said to give me a day or two, and we'd figure something out.

Clint took my hand and said he hoped a day or two wouldn't be too late.

Saturday May 19

As promised, Clint was terminated at work. He was afraid to stay at the Lawson any longer. Wise choice. He said if his mother followed through with her threats and told his father, people would come here to get him.

"People we don't want to see."

Who? I have no idea if he was being overly dramatic or not.

Clint told me to go into work and act as though nothing out of the ordinary was happening. He was asking a great deal. Clint said he would hide out somewhere. When I asked him where, he just shrugged. He scared me with all this talk.

I went down the hall and knocked on Max's door. He opened it a crack. He still looked like hell. If anything, his eye appeared even worse. Greens and yellows had emerged where the purple had begun to fade. Max said he couldn't go in to work. The owner of the Silver Chalice was understanding, but told him diners didn't want to see him until he was fully healed. He said he wished he was getting paid for the time off.

Clint and I ducked inside Max's room, and I gave him a quick synopsis of everything that was going on. He said Clint could stay there for the day. "What are they going to do, ruin my life? They're a little late with that threat." Max said it as a joke, but not really. When Max asked who his parents were that wielded such power, Clint said his father was General _____. Wow, one of Eisenhower's top advisors and now a Cold War kingpin in US/Soviet relations. Until that moment, I had no idea.

Holy shit.

Boy the thought of having that man, the *Bulldog of the Battlefield*, as an enemy terrified me. I tried to be calm and not let it show. I thanked Max profusely and told Clint I'd try to be home early from work. We'd figure out our next move then. I sounded braver and more assured than I was. I wondered briefly if all this was worth it, but only briefly. Clint was reason enough. He was worth anything and everything. Love gave me a strength I never knew I possessed. I'd muster whatever courage I would need. I was tired of being beaten down and living in fear.

Sunday May 20

Yesterday seemed endless. All day at work, I wondered how Clint was faring and if he had been discovered in Max's room. Everyone at M_____ seemed to be acting strangely, as though they knew more than they did. Was I just being paranoid? Were they responding to my distracted behavior? Nothing seemed quite right, or quite as it should be. I wondered what sort of excuse had been given for Clint's abrupt termination. I was sure Ella was talking about it. Whispering. Gossiping. Conjecturing.

Nobody mentioned anything to me, which was suspicious as well. Most of them usually shot their bazoos off about everything in loud and unashamed voices. Not today. Why?

Throughout the day and even on the walk home, I couldn't help but wonder if I was being followed, watched. Everyone looked suspicious or stared a bit too long. Boy, but the thought of it all gave me the jitters. I was about out of my skin by the time I got back to the Lawson.

Who was that man reading in the lobby?

Why were there so many gentlemen here that I'd never seen before?

Was that normal?

Was I typically that unaware?

I had to get a grip on myself and my thoughts. I wasn't going to do anyone any good in this state.

Clint and I slept in Max's room that night, and Max took mine. I told him it might be dangerous. Max said he didn't care. He reiterated he had nothing left to lose. Over the course of the day, his black eye had yellowed even more. He tried to downplay the danger and change the subject. Max asked me if I'd seen Marilyn singing *Happy Birthday* at President Kennedy's birthday party. I said no. He said it was the sexiest thing he'd seen outside of a burlesque house. Max told me it was all over TV.

Clint and I have to make some decisions. Clint maintains he isn't going to be ordered about by his father anymore. Given the circumstances and his father's position, that is a huge statement. *Huge!* He said his father needs to realize that although he's a general on the battlefield, he has no right to issue mandates and commands in everyday life. "He's a dictator. They both are," Clint said, before adding that he only wanted me. "No one else's approval matters to me. I only want to be with you, Joseph. Nothing else matters." I wondered for a moment if Clint wanted me for me, or because I gave him the strength to defy his circumstances. I couldn't let my insecurities take hold. Those roots had strangled me before. I had to believe him. That was essential. Besides, don't we always love the people we do for the things they bring out in us? For giving us strength? For making us greater than we were?

Clint said he wanted us to run away. I told him it wouldn't be easy. We'd be two men together, hiding from not only a powerful family, but also from the Army. My heart raced at the thought of it all. A combination of fear and excitement. The army did not take kindly to young men who failed to show up for boot camp.

Clint shook his head. "That isn't how my father works. He's too proud to get the military involved in something like this. He'll do anything to avoid a scandal. Anything. However, he will not be adverse to calling out his spies."

"Spies?"

Clint said to forget he said anything. "The less you know the better…" Clint said he needed to work out to clear his head. I told him it was too risky here. He couldn't argue with my logic. We had to get out. We left the Lawson by the back exit and went to the Triumph Gym in the South Loop. Clint had heard things about this place. When I asked what sort of things, Clint just smiled. The Italian fellow at the front desk gave Clint a long stare, making no attempt to disguise his attraction. Seems Clint had heard right.. We were among friends here.

Clint found some new admirers among the gym's clientele. He'd heard a lot of men who frequented the place were attracted to bodybuilders. *Connoisseurs*. Working out, Clint was attracting them left and right. Between sets at the bench press, Clint told one of his especially ardent fans that we were in a jam. The man, Rick, said he could spend the night at his place.

"We," said Clint, looking over at me.

The man sneered in my direction.

The way he stared at Clint made it clear strings were firmly attached. This favor came with a price. The guy wanted something for the inconvenience. Clint was willing. I had to rise above my jealousy and see the bigger picture. Love isn't always the way they describe it in fairy tales. Clint was doing this for us. Suddenly it became evident that my life, our lives, had turned a corner. The rules of love had just expanded to include new kinds of compromise. Survival on this level meant greater sacrifice. From now on, we had to do whatever was necessary to be together.

When they left to go back to Rick's place, I snuck back to the Lawson to get our things. I asked Clint if he wanted anything specific from his room. Clint shook his head and kissed me hard. He looked into my eyes and said he already had everything he needed. I loved him more for that. Somehow that made his going off with Rick not seem so awful. At the Lawson, I packed some clothes and papers from his desk in one bag and my things in another. What couldn't fit into the suitcases, I gave to Max. He said he'd put it in storage and wished us well. There were tears in his eyes. He said he would miss me. Max had become a true friend.

Tomorrow is my day off. Tomorrow I am going to the bank first thing, withdraw my savings, and close my checking account. I have enough money to give us a fresh start somewhere. On his last day at work, Clint had cashed his paycheck. Earlier today, he talked to the men at the gym about picking up extra cash. *Modeling work.* They said they could hook him up with some people in New York. More connoisseurs. *Physical culture enthusiasts.* We both knew what he would have to do, but being together and escaping was all that mattered.

Monday May 21

Another day in hiding. Rick has his motives for letting us stay with him. He likes Clint to start in a posing strap and then work out nude for him. Rick likes to watch and take pictures. He has gym equipment in his basement. He likes Clint to flex for him. Rick likes to oil him up. Rick assured Clint the camera didn't have any film in it, and Clint believed him. I have my doubts.

Big picture.

Rick says he goes to Triumph Gym to see the muscle boys sweat. Lucky for us, Rick has his own agenda and doesn't care about much else. I asked Clint if he was okay with doing all this. He blushed and said he likes the click of the camera. He gets hard posing for Rick. "His desire sparks mine, but it is just a game. Different from what we have. Ours isn't a game. Ours is real."

I need to remember that.

We are leaving here tomorrow. Can't say I'm sorry. A little bit of this Rick situation goes a long way. He's a lecher and a creep. He's a connoisseur who'd like to devour my lover. I thought I would be okay with all of it, but I'm really not. Jealousy can be fickle. Part of me is jealous of Rick and part of me is envious of Clint. I want Clint's sole attention, and yet I want to ignite the same desire that Clint ignites in others. I've heard it said that we lust after what we wish for in ourselves.

I'm exhausted and talking nonsense. I suspect things will be more of the same in New York, but who knows? The wisest course of action seems to head north into

Canada, out of the country, and hopefully out of the reach of Clint's father, the Army, and the "band of spies." Was Clint exaggerating about that?

I'm afraid to even ask.

I don't know what awaits us in Canada, but we'll be together. We have to keep focusing on that. Being together is the main thing. Being together is everything. The outside world is unimportant as long as I'm with Clint. Life finally has a focus. When I look into Clint's eyes, everything makes sense.

Tuesday May 22

This is really happening. I never thought I'd be leaving everything I know behind, but I never expected Clint to come into my life. At some point, being hopeful became being delusional. Then the impossible happened.

With Clint, it is suddenly clear how little everything else matters, and how effortlessly the skin of my previous life can be shed. With Clint, I have found my peace even in the midst of this chaos. With Clint, I have found my home.

I turned the last page in the journal Joseph had written. Springtime 1962 was over. The writing ended, but I knew his story must have continued. The tale of Joseph and Clint obviously did not end there. I needed, hungered to hear more. The journal had spoken to me of love as no novel or verse ever had done. This tale filled me with hope that the right man for me was out there somewhere, but he simply had yet to come along. And when he did, everything would be different. Transformative. After all, something similar had happened to Joseph.

The following day, I took the Clark Street bus to Epic Reads to search for additional materials. There had to be something more about the couple's adventures. The same bell greeted me as I entered the shop. A different person was sitting behind the counter. He had his nose buried in a book. Once again, classical music played from the radio at the back of the store. Nothing seemed to have been moved or shifted since my previous visit, as evidenced by the additional layer of dust coating everything. If another volume of Joseph's journal existed, logic dictated it would be shelved near where I had found the first one. When I walked down the stacks, the same cat jumped from an upper shelf and startled me. The man at the front desk heard me gasp and bellowed, "You okay?" I replied that I was fine.

I located the bottom shelf below the haphazard stack of mysteries. Certain this was the place where I'd found the Springtime 1962 journal, I perused several scrapbooks. The items in this area certainly looked promising. I flipped through a 1970s family's car vacation in Oregon and Washington. I looked through Bob and Karen's wedding album, Love Forever—but if that was the case, why had their wedding album ended up at a used bookstore? I needed to find the subsequent Joseph and Clint journal. I was becoming far too cynical.

I was starting to worry I wasn't going to find an additional diary when I saw a composition book identical to the first at the end of the row. I held my breath as I opened it. Before the notebook actually began, there were a number of sheets stapled to the front cover. Every page was filled with the handwriting I'd come to know so well. This one was labeled Autumn 1962. My heart raced as I realized I was holding another volume of Joseph and Clint's story. I checked but didn't see anything more.

I was trembling with excitement as I made my way to the counter with my treasure. The total was $1.25. Since it was raining, I asked for a plastic bag.

I bought a bottle of wine at the liquor store across from my apartment. There was no mail. The hallway smelled like someone was having fish for dinner. I flipped the deadbolt of the door as I entered. The cat greeted me. Nothing on the answering machine. Typical. I poured myself a glass of Merlot and stretched out on the sofa. Home and safe and happy at last. With an anticipatory sigh, I opened the journal labeled Autumn 1962 and began to read the irregular sheets stapled to the front cover. The sheets of stapled paper were actually titled Summer 1962.

Wednesday May 23

We left Rick's place just before dawn. I was eager to get out of there. I didn't like sharing Clint with the likes of Rick, but necessity sometimes dictates. We were desperate and low on options. Clint said if he knew his father, the General probably had his goons already looking for us. He called his father relentless.

We pooled our money and had two suitcases worth of belongings. Most importantly, we had each other. We debated leaving by plane or bus or train. I asked Clint which his father would suspect. He said he'd suspect them all. Apparently that was why he was a top general. When I asked what he wouldn't expect, Clint said, "Anything else." Then that was what we had to do.

I asked if Clint knew anyone who would help us, someone we could trust. Clint mentioned an ex, a fellow named Graves who lived on Diversey. I asked if Graves had a car. Clint nodded and said he did when he knew him, "But that was last year." Apparently Graves told Clint to give him a call if he ever needed anything. I doubt this was what Graves had in mind, but as I said, our options were limited. Clint said there was no animosity between them that he knew of. There was a phone booth on the corner. Clint was reading my mind.

Clint said Graves wasn't thrilled to hear from him. Understandable. I imagined Graves had been gaga for Clint, and then things had ended. I put myself in his shoes. Easy to imagine how devastating that would be. The need to be aloof made sense. Who wants to get hurt again? And who wants to get a phone call from a former lover and his new boyfriend needing help? Graves must be a nice guy. He told us to come right over. Clint and I took the train to the Fullerton CTA stop and walked to Graves's studio flat.

A handsome young man with wavy red hair opened the door. Graves and Clint embraced and exchanged niceties. Clint introduced me. Graves sized me up. I could tell my age threw him. He was cordial. Graves asked if we wanted breakfast. Clint shook his head and said we were in a jam. He briefly explained.

"Shit," was all Graves had to say.

Clint asked if we could use his car, but Graves needed it. Clint asked if he could give us a ride. That was what we'd wanted all along, but sometimes getting what you want is easier if the person you ask thinks you want something more. Manipulation pure and simple. Clint asked if he'd drive us to Milwaukee or the Quad Cities or even Rockford. "Please," he added. Graves relented. I suspect he's still in love with Clint. Graves called in sick to work and grabbed his keys. We were out the door in five minutes.

We took the stairs to street level. His salmon 1958 Impala two-door was parked on Pine Grove. "Nice car," I said. Graves said it had been his mother's. She'd had a stroke last July.

Graves took us to Rockford. A ninety minute drive overall. The Impala rode like a charm. Plenty of time to chat. Graves seemed a decent fellow. If I were in his shoes, I'm not sure I would have been so accommodating. Graves was an artist. Supposedly they're more sensitive. Compassionate. Two years ago, Graves had painted Clint. A classic physique study series. Clint answered an ad in the paper for Models Wanted. That was how they met. I said painting Clint in a posing strap would make me fall in love with him, too. Graves said there was no strap. They were together almost a year. When the draft came, Clint was off to school. Both decided it was best to end things. Clean. No ties. By the catch in Graves's voice, I could tell the decision hadn't been mutual. Maybe it was Constance? Clearly, Graves was still carrying a torch. He said he hadn't dated anyone seriously since then.

I caught Graves eying me several times during the drive as if thinking, "Why him? Why this middle-aged man?" I ask myself the same thing every day. Maybe in the future, something will happen to break us up as well. Then I, too, will only be another of Clint's ex-lovers.

Clint had Graves drop us off on State Street in downtown Rockford. We both thanked him. When Graves wished us good luck, his eyes were teary. I stood on the curb while Clint and Graves spoke briefly. I was beginning to get impatient when they kissed and shared an extended hug. Clint got out of the car. I wanted to ask him what Graves had said but reminded myself it was none of my business. I had a fairly good idea. Besides, I think Clint likes my restraint. Mustn't undo my reputation. I had my pride.

We walked a couple blocks up the street to the bus station. The next departure for Minneapolis was midnight. That left us with a full day to kill. We stowed our gear in a depot locker and wondered what to do for the next twelve hours. The Four Horseman of the Apocalypse with Glenn Ford was playing down the street. A darkened theater provided some safety. Walking around might attract attention. We were still too close to Chicago for my comfort. I paid the dollar admission. We sat through the picture twice, and it was almost two and a half hours. Not exactly my cup of tea, but that was okay.

We were able to get some sleep. We napped in shifts. The balcony at the Midway Theater in Rockford featured some of the same doings as I'd seen in Chicago. The signals for a bit of play looked much the same but were carried out a bit more cautiously. I explored while Clint slept. Sometimes watching is even better than doing. I've always been a bit of a voyeur.

When we left the theater, the sun was low to the west. Everything seemed to stand in relief in that rose and orange glow. Surreal. The buildings looked like a film set, a false front of plaster and painted boards. Love that time of day.

When we returned to the depot lot, we noticed two men in suits at the front counter. Clint pulled me back from the window. He didn't like the look of them. Detectives. Private Investigators. MPs. Clint said he knew that type on sight. Same haircut. Same shoes. I wondered if he was being paranoid. I had to trust his judgment. We ducked around the back of the building. They didn't see us. The clerk from earlier was still on duty at the front desk. We wondered how much she would tell or if she'd remember us asking about the midnight bus to Minneapolis. All at once I noticed Clint's distraction.

A man in tight dungarees and a checkered shirt leaned against a 1958 Buick Super. He took a drag off his smoke, gave Clint a slow head to toe, and nodded for us to come over. He asked if we were looking for a ride. He was saying "we," but was talking just to my boyfriend. I was all but invisible. Clint said yes, we were looking for a ride. The man asked if we were willing to pay, and Clint gave him a holding stare. He said we were short on funds, but that we'd be happy to barter. I wondered where Clint had learned all this banter. Was it instinctual? The man introduced himself as John. Clint asked John if he could do us a favor first. He asked me for the locker key and asked John to get our gear. "There's some fellows in there we aren't too anxious to see." John didn't ask why. He didn't ask any questions at all, just nodded, flicked his cigarette, took the key, and went inside. As soon as he was out of earshot, I told Clint I didn't trust him. Clint told me to relax. Clint said if we wanted to get out of this, that we had to take chances. Calculated risks, was how he phrased it.

Thursday May 24

John isn't really John. His name is Leo. He said he introduces himself as John out of habit. He knows a lot of people in the area. "Rockford is no Chicago," was what he said by way of an explanation. "It's dangerous here." I should've said Chicago can be brutal for our kind too, but he was never really talking to me. Every word was directed at Clint. No surprise when Leo and Clint messed around last night.

Clint said that's just the way things were. Reality. Some things I just need to accept. I decided that if I saw the goings-on that I saw today at the Midway, I'd go from being a voyeur to a participant. What's good for the goose, I figured. I covered my head with the pillow, but I could still hear them.

Leo lives with his mother in a run-down place on the west side. The porch was rotten and sloped. The inside of the house smelled of fried bologna and cigarettes. Leo told his mother that Clint was a friend of his technical school. And that I was Clint's dad. Boy but that hurt, and judging from his smirk, I presume that was Leo's intent. He is an asshole. After the introduction, his mother mumbled, "Pleased to meet you" before shuffling back into the kitchen. She switched on the radio and took a bottle from the cabinet. With a ragged cough, she settled in a chair. Leo said she was a drunk. Didn't bother to lower his voice. She knows what she is. He said she was that way ever since his dad left. Clint asked him when that was, and Leo said before he was born. Leo said she didn't use a glass anymore. That was how he knew she was alcoholic. He claimed having her be a drunk made things easier. "She doesn't remember anything, except things that happened years ago. She figures she imagines the rest. She doesn't even ask about the men that come and go. I tell her everyone is a friend from technical school." I suspected his mother knew more than Leo supposed.

Leo made us popcorn but put soy sauce on it instead of salt and butter. Better than it sounds. We all had beers and watched Dr. Kildare in the living room. His mother was humming to herself in the kitchen through half the episode. I was distracted for a thousand different reasons.

Clint slept on the couch. I slept on the living room floor.

Friday May 25

Leo worked today. When Clint asked what sort of work he did, Leo said he does stuff for his uncle. He doesn't like to get his hands dirty. I wasn't sure if Leo was speaking metaphorically or not. I didn't want to know.

Leo is one of those guys who claims that family is everything, yet he's clearly resentful of that importance. He treats his mother horribly. Abusively. He was yelling at her this morning. She was distraught. Claimed she'd seen a second ghost. I looked at Clint, and he looked at me. A second one. Did she mean us? Leo started shouting at her. Calling her names. Most of what he yelled was indecipherable. He sounded crazy. Excessive. Out of control. Maybe living with an alcoholic day in and day out does that to a person eventually. Still. His mother didn't say a word in response.

Before heading out, Leo peeked his head into the living room and said he'd be back around two o'clock. We heard his mother crying about the second ghost after he left. Eerie. We stared at each other. There was nothing to do in a situation like that except become ghosts ourselves. Disappear. Eventually we heard the clatter of bottles behind her bedroom door. Maybe she was eager to forget.

A few minutes later, I got up and made coffee. I knocked on her door. No answer. I asked if she wanted coffee. She screamed No. The rage of her answer startled me. Frightening. She's a deeply troubled woman. Clint and I had our coffee on the back porch. The yard was quiet except for the birds. Now and then, we heard sounds from her room above the porch. Boy, I am eager to get the hell out of here. I told Clint I half expected to be attacked in our sleep. Clint felt the same way. This setup gave us both the creeps. Clint mimicked the theme from Psycho.

Clint said that was his favorite motion picture. When he asked mine, I said I didn't know. Funny the things we've discussed and the things we haven't. My favorite films change with my mood. When he pressed me, I named a few: Some Like it Hot, Bundle of Joy, Laura, The Narrow Margin, Gentlemen Prefer Blondes, A Foreign Affair, Cheaper By The Dozen, My Man Godfrey, The Seven Year Itch, Vertigo… Finally he said, "okay okay" and started laughing. When I went to get a refill of coffee, she was in the kitchen. Standing in the shadows. Her eyes were dark and red and ringed. She scared the hell out of me. I sloshed the partial cup of coffee in my hand. When I moved to clean it up, she stared a moment longer before shuffling out of the room. Clint came inside during the tail end of her lunacy. I told him I wanted to get out of here. Today.

We came back in and turned on the television. I hadn't watched game shows in forever. Concentration. Camouflage. Truth or Consequences. We flipped the channel. Scott Carpenter and Project Mercury were all over the news. The Aurora 7 orbited the earth three times.

Leo came home at a little after one. Never thought I'd be happy to see him, but I admit I was relieved. Clint told him we needed to get going. Leo said he likes to drive and was eager to take the Buick on a road trip. He didn't have anything to do for his uncle tomorrow. He'd be glad to take us someplace. Clint said he'd be appreciative. They went up to Leo's room after that. I'd be a fool not to know what was going on. Afterward, Clint came back down to the living room. He spent the night with me. I am so anxious to leave here. Tomorrow cannot come soon enough.

First Rick. Now Leo. I think Clint likes being a commodity. I suppose it affirms his self-worth. He's hardly the untrained youth I first thought him to be. He's so much more. I'm learning new things about him every day. Interesting how my view of him has changed. Grown richer. Clint has gone from being a dream come true to being a beautiful but complex person. I suppose we all are more than what we seem.

During the night, we heard an awful row upstairs. Leo and his mother were at it again. Shouts. Cussing. I hated hearing stuff like that, it reminded me of when I was a kid. No specific memory, simply a primitive feeling of being unsafe. Unsure. Of knowing I needed to keep my wits about me. Sleep was impossible.

Saturday May 26

At the crack of dawn, Leo stuck his head in the living room and called for us to wake up. I was already awake. He was taking us to Detroit. He said it without looking at me. He was too busy checking out Clint's morning erection. A lewd smile. Drooling. Seconds later, a matching bulge at Leo's crotch. He looked over as though he was expecting me to flee the room. Think again. He'd messed around with my boyfriend enough. Let him hate me. I didn't care, as long as he was our ticket out of here.

Leo couldn't go farther than Detroit because of his mom. He had to be back around sundown or soon after because sometimes her drinking causes problems. Incidents. "Sometimes she imagines things, especially at night." Ghosts. I could only guess what went on in her gin-soaked mind beneath this roof when Leo and his mother were alone. The thought gave me chills. Depressing and frightening in equal measure.

True to his word, Leo had us on the road in less than an hour. I was in the backseat, of course. The chaperone. The third wheel. Leo drove like a teenager out to impress. He pressed on the gas until the speedometer topped eighty, and I remember thinking that we were all going to end up wrapped around a power pole like Ernie Kovacs.

When Leo ran in to pee at a rest stop, I got a chance to share a private word with Clint. He seems to think Leo is okay. Clint said not to worry. "I know how to handle men like Leo." Sure I was jealous. But despite my feelings, Leo was a queer duck. I suppose being raised by a drunk gave you a strange view of the world. And not much guidance in how to behave in civilized company. I kept all additional doubts to myself. We'd be free of him by dusk. Still, Leo seemed to be hiding plenty. But I suppose we're all hiding something. Maybe with a home life like that, he just has more to hide than most. Maybe those ghosts were real.

Sunday May 27

Glad yesterday is over. The entire ride, past cornfields and wheat fields, I could tell something was brewing with Leo. As we approached the Detroit city limits, Leo took an exit into a suburban shopping district and parked in a Sears lot. He said he needed to talk to Clint for a few minutes. A clue for me to get lost. I went for a root beer and said I'd be back in a bit. Leo said to make it an hour. Clint said he'd see me then. He put extra emphasis on the word then. I couldn't tell if he was asking me not to be late or not to come back a minute earlier. Same thing and yet very different. Did he want to play with Leo, or did he want to be saved? Maybe both.

I gave Leo five dollars and said at thirty cents a gallon that should go a long way toward filling his tank. He gave it back to me. "I don't want your money." The way he said it made it clear to me I had something he did want. Clint, I presumed. I was nervous leaving those two alone. I trusted Clint, but I sure didn't trust Leo. Part of me worried they wouldn't be there when I got back in an hour.

When I returned, Clint was leaning against a light post with our bags at his feet. As it happened, Leo was looking for more than sex. He asked Clint point blank what he was doing with me. Leo told Clint he'd be happier with him. Leo said they could live with his mom… or without her. I wondered what that was supposed to mean. Clint told Leo no. He wasn't interested. Wish I could have seen Leo's face when he said that! Clint said nothing more about the exchange.

My guess is that Leo took off in that baby blue Buick Super with a squeal of rubber.

"He said to say good-bye."

Like heck he did.

Clint took my hand. We were near the Canadian border. We should've kept moving, but I was suddenly so hungry for him. I'd doubted him, and I'd doubted us. I'd feared love would prove me a fool and I'd be betrayed at the first opportunity. But it hadn't happened. Such a relief to have my fears unfounded. The stress of running, of escape seems to be getting to us. Or me. I'm not young or a thrill seeker. I don't crave excitement. I was in love. For the first time in my life, it seemed I was wanted. The bad part was, I was a wanted man in more ways than one. Other things were bothering me as well. Sharing Clint with others makes me want him more. Makes me want to prove to him every time we make love that I'm the one. This stuff didn't bother him. He told me monogamy was a trap. Conventional. He saw love and sex as two different things. Clint said if I didn't understand that, maybe we weren't meant to be together. A veiled threat? Youthful bravado? Sometimes young people see the world so differently.

I told Clint I need to be reassured sometimes. Feel special. Loved. Adored. Clint asked what would convince me. His grin made it clear he knew what I needed. Am I so shallow? Sometimes, yes. Gladly and blessedly shallow. Clint can be so cocky. I should be angry, but all that confidence strikes me as charming. Assured. Something I so often lack. Clint wanted me to say what I needed. Express my desire for him. He wanted me to tell him graphically. He wanted me to say I wanted his cock, that I wanted his cock inside me.

He winked and suggested we find a place for the night.

We rented a room a few blocks from the highway. The proprietor thought we were father and son. Though it made things easier, the assumption was hell on my ego. Inside the room, I threw a red handkerchief over the bedside lamp. A trick from a movie. Presto! The room became a bordello. I laid on the bed and told Clint to get undressed. I was aroused before his belt was unbuckled. So beautiful. Confident. Knowing every second the effect he was having upon me. A hairy Rory Calhoun. Built. He slipped off his underwear. I got off the bed and crawled across the carpet on my knees. Make me beg. Make me show you how I worship you. He knew where this fantasy was going, and he was more than willing to comply. What man doesn't love to be adored?

For the next hour, I worshipped him with my tongue. I started with his toes. Up his torso. Salty. My tongue's trail was long and lasting until finally I licked and tickled his ears. That drove him wild. I kissed his temples. His hairline. Ran my tongue down the side of his cheek, under his chin, and down his jawline. Across the hollows of his arms. Hairy pungent pits. Out to his fingertips before licking back toward his torso on the underside. Skin. So much beautiful skin. Pliant with youth. Tanned. I planted kisses down the furry trail to his waist and around to the firm globes of his buttocks. Melons. Hairy. Muscular. Dimpled. Grand. I parted them, licking slowly, and finally lips on his rectum. Grinding to meet my tongue. Reaching to pull my head closer. Moaning when I licked hip bone to his genitals. His member was rock hard. Flush to his belly. Squatting on my haunches. Seeking only to serve. With a sexy and confident smile, he ran a thumb around my lips. The slightest of nods. I swallowed his manhood. More. Faster. Sucking. Faster. The spray on the back of my throat. Continuing until I felt him deflate. Eventually he collapsed upon me, heavy and spent. Once more, he is mine.

He called me the best and kissed me. That was what I longed to hear. Needed to hear. At that moment, I vowed to do whatever it took to keep hearing those words. I knew no indignity when it came to love. Not after waiting so long.

Clint fell asleep soon after. I turned on the television. James Cagney and Joan Blondell on the Late Movie. I held Clint in my arms and made lazy circles in the fur of his chest. Kissed his head. So beautiful. Angelic. Demonic. Perfect and warm. I'd fantasized about men like this all my life. Possessing and being possessed by them. Now my dream had come true. How the hell had a fantasy become real? Content in the glow of the television. Cagney kissed Blondell, and I smiled. Once more, Clint was mine without question.

Monday May 28

Catching our breath. Reconnecting. We need a plan. Clint was restless for a workout and headed out to find a gym. I sat around the room. Read a book from the lobby shelf, The Young Lions by Irwin Shaw. Three different views of WWII from the perspective of three very different men. Liked the theme. Clever. True. Point of view really is everything. The book took me out of myself and these present circumstances. For a while anyway. Diversion. That's all anything is anymore, a diversion.

Late in the afternoon, I opened the curtain. Counted the windows on the office building across the street. Counted a second time. My mind wandered. I counted the windows on the apartments on the other side of the road. I decided I'd buy a deck of cards tomorrow. An underground essential.

Clint returned around dinnertime. Quiet and withdrawn. Said he had a good workout. The reason for his odd mood was a mystery. Maybe there was no reason. Sometimes people simply are who they are from moment to moment. I wasn't going to pester him with questions. Clint lay down for a bit and seemed more like himself after a nap. Maybe he'd been nothing more than tired.

We walked down near the highway and ducked into a diner for the fried chicken special. Then walked around to help with digestion and stopped for an ice-cream cone. When we got back to the room, we turned on the TV. Clint was asleep in five minutes. The Linda Darnell picture they showed on the Late Show was awful, but I watched every implausible minute of it nonetheless.

Tuesday May 29

More of the same. Clint disappeared again for most of the day. Maybe this is nothing at all. He needs space. Quite plausible I'm just discovering how much space he needs. Everyone needs some time alone. That's in our DNA.

I walked around the city. Never been to Detroit before. Certainly has its charm. Lake St. Clair. The Detroit River. Some beautiful churches. The Jefferson corridor area is certainly grand and the Kean is a handsome building. I window-shopped and was pleased I remembered to buy a deck of cards. Despite the charm of the architecture and topography, my mind was wandering to Clint and our dilemma. Was there a dilemma? We needed to talk this evening. If not about us, then about the future. We were living in a fool's paradise without some sort of plan. Having no plan was planning for capture.

Back in our room. Ten games of solitaire. Won two.

Later: For reasons unknown, Clint seems reluctant to make plans about our next move. What is going on? My dark imagination wonders if he is meeting someone during the time when he is supposedly working out. Having second thoughts? Thinking of leaving? I hate to be overly possessive or insecure, but something is amiss. I don't want to be confrontational because I'm afraid he'll leave me. I don't think I could endure that. I have no bargaining chip. He holds all the cards and has all the power. He keeps asking why I am looking at him. I know my staring is getting on his nerves, yet I can't help it. I keep thinking I can solve this. Solve him. Save us. Maybe I'm the one who's in the strange mood. These four walls are making me crazy.

Lying in the dark, I said I was sorry. Explained that I get nervous without a plan or direction. He said maybe we should think of a way to stay here for a while. Odd comment. Here? Detroit? I suggested we cross the border to Canada. So close. He seemed agreeable to that. I thought that was the plan all along. Maybe I was mistaken. Or presumed that we'd decided on this.

I never thought I'd leave my country. I'd pledged allegiance to it for decades. I'd bought war bonds and swore there was no place better on earth. I'd never even been out of the US before and only out of my time zone twice. (This was the second time.) I love America dearly, but I love Clint more. If being together means leaving the country, I'll do it in a heartbeat. My new allegiance is to Clint. To love.

Wednesday May 30

Getting out of the country is looking to be more complicated than we supposed. We still don't have a plan, but we do have a direction and that has made all the difference. I'm confident we'll find a solution if we focus on our problem. So far that hasn't happened.

This morning Clint did push-ups on the motel room floor until he was covered in sweat. The interplay of muscles on his back hypnotized me. I love the smell of him. Sweet tangy perspiration. The pulse of his veins when he flexes his biceps made me weak. He lay on top of me, covering me with his mass. A delicious smothering. He took me right there on the bed with his sweat as lubrication. Afterward, we shared a bottle of wine. I bathed him by candlelight. He closed his eyes and asked me to read to him. I picked up By Love Possessed by James Cozzens, which was on the nightstand. He said he loved the sound of my voice. His sex floated heavy in the water. When it began to thicken, he grabbed me and pulled me into the tub. He kissed me hard and guided my hand to his penis. Fully erect in no time. We made love again. This time he took me on the bathroom floor. Frantic. Fevered. Careless. Glorious. I hoped we didn't make too much noise. The libido of a young lover is a wonderful magical thing. I have scratches and scrapes from the tile as well as a bruise where my knee whacked the toilet. Marks of love. Battle scars for my beloved. How could I have doubted Clint? How could I have doubted us? How could I have doubted this?

I poured us each a glass with the last of the wine as we moved to the bed. Clint tuned the motel radio in to a country station. When I said I didn't realize he liked that kind of music, he said it depended on his mood. "Like me and movies," I laughed. He nodded. "Like us," he replied. Wasn't sure what he meant by that, but the moment was too nice to complicate with more talk or explanations.

We drifted to sleep in one another's arms. This was our best evening since fleeing Chicago. Tonight I remembered why we were doing this and why it was worth risking everything. We were doing it to stay together. There was no debating the worth of our togetherness. I need to remember that. Study it. Love isn't easy, but it's better than loneliness.

Thursday May 31

Clint has been soliciting himself to maintain our income. He told me today when he saw my expression after he said he was going to work out. He said he would've told me, but he knew I'd just worry. He told me he liked doing it.

"I don't like hurting you, but it turns me on to have men paying me, to see a man that hungry."

What could I say? No? Forbid him? Deny him from doing what gave him pleasure. I knew Clint better than that. Telling him no wouldn't stop him, it would only cause resentment. Drive a wedge between us. Telling him no would be the start of his wanting to leave me. Needing his freedom. No was never a good word to hear from one's beloved. Instead, I said it was risky. "If you get nabbed, this is all over."

He nodded. "I'll be careful." I hoped to God that was true.

They announced today that 90 percent of American homes now own a television set. Hard to imagine how people got along before TV. But we managed just fine. Heaven forbid people should have to make conversation or learn to entertain themselves. I fear one day we won't even know how to make conversation anymore. Sometimes I sound like such a grumpy old man. I was so much older before I met Clint.

Later: When Clint came back to the room today, he said he was ready to get a real job. Not sure what happened or if anything happened. He didn't hint at either. I'd like to think he realized how much his behavior was bothering me. That's what I would like to think, but so much of Clint is a mystery to me. Strange how you can know someone so well in some ways, but not in others. The why of his decision is unimportant. I'm just glad that chapter is closed for now.

Friday June 1

Space travel has people being launched into the atmosphere, the farthest reaches known to man… and yet, here we are, stuck in Detroit. We've been here a week now. We need to get moving, to flee without leaving a trail. Detroit is not bad, but it's not home.

The good news is we managed to find free lodging here with proper jobs for both of us. Well, if we are working for lodging, I guess it isn't free, but it's welcome nonetheless. Maybe Detroit is a sort of home, at least for the time being.

We were talking to the waitress at a coffee shop about finding work, and not five minutes later, a man came up to our booth and introduced himself. Giovanni turned to Clint and said he was looking for someone to help with landscaping. "Worst it ever will be is removing some tree stumps or hedges. Mostly, it's mowing lawns, putting in a rock garden. Rock gardens are big this summer," he said.

Afterward, Clint wondered aloud why Giovanni had asked him. I looked at him like he was daft. "The waitress probably mentioned us looking for work and Giovanni saw you sitting there, muscled and fit in your T-shirt." I laughed, "Like you could pull out a tree stump with your teeth." Clint blushed. He knew I was right. Maybe he just wanted to hear me say it.

Giovanni gave Clint the pay rate and said he had solid work for three weeks, maybe more. He said for half the wage we could live in his attic. Giovanni turned to me and asked what I could do. Evidently I don't seem the landscaping type. I said I could wash cars and clean, paint a house.

He asked if I knew Latin. In fact, I do. Wasn't expecting that. Giovanni's daughter, Catherine, needs a tutor. She'd done poorly in the language during the school year. Evidently her subpar performance bothers him. Giovanni is an immigrant and a widower. He is determined that his daughter is going to get the best education possible.

We moved our things from the motel over to Giovanni's home later in the afternoon. Work for both of us begins tomorrow.

Saturday June 2

All it took was talking for an hour or so with Catherine to discover that the reason she has such difficulty in Latin is because she is smitten by a boy named Anthony who sits next to her in class. Latin isn't difficult, but it does require attention and memorization, but Anthony makes paying attention impossible. A poor grade in Latin is not Catherine's deepest concern. Amidst a flood of tears, she said Anthony didn't know that she is alive.

The arrangement here is working out nicely. Giovanni suspects nothing between Clint and I. To him, we're a pair of drifters. And I suppose from one perspective, that's precisely what we are. He's typical in that regard. Most people don't see us as more. I'm dumbfounded that the intense love I feel for Clint is mostly invisible to the general populace. Most people only seem to see love in familiar forms. Like only being able to discern certain colors on a spectrum. Giovanni has never questioned what Clint and I are doing together. I'm grateful we don't have to lie.

Monday June 4

I've spent the past few days earning my pay as a Latin teacher, but the vast majority of the time has been spent counseling a lovelorn girl. Strange to think of love as that uncomplicated. Given my current circumstances, a world where love involves only the feelings between two people sounds so nice. Some couples don't have that luxury: a Jew in love with a Christian, a Catholic in love with a Methodist, a Black in love with a White, or two women, or two men. All taboo. Unacceptable. Insidious. Often outsider love has more to do with the knots and thorns than it does with the rose.

Life can be hard when you only have each other. Clint is exhausted at the end of the day. Giovanni works him hard, making sure he's getting the most for his money. Clint's workday begins at five thirty in the morning, and he is asleep by eight thirty at night. This family has no books, so I wandered down to the used bookstore at the end of the street and pawed through the nickel paperback bin. Chandler and Cain, Ellery Queen, Mickey Spillane, and Erle Stanley Gardner—all for a quarter. The bookstore has been my daily excursion. When I return, Catherine does her lessons and I read. We work a bit on vocabulary, she recites her translation to me, we discuss her mistakes, and then we're through. Afterward, I read in the backyard. Giovanni isn't rich, but the family has a yard and a hammock.

Getting bored with all this, but I need to accept that it's all part of living underground. Hiding is exciting in some ways and mundane in others. Limiting. When you're hiding, the only thrill comes from the possibility of being found. In our case, a terrifying thought. Our love has been on the back burner for a while. We can't risk any sexual activity here. That's done nothing for my mood. I fear we're losing sight of things. Clint drags himself in the house at the end of the day, and I worry he's beginning to resent all this. Maybe it's all my imagination. Maybe I'm the resentful one.

When Clint got home from work, I told him we needed a night out. Time alone. We ended up going to see The Road to Hong Kong with Hope, Crosby, and Lamour… and Joan Collins along for the ride this time. Clint had never seen a Road film before. At times like this, our age difference rears its ugly head. I'd always enjoyed Crosby/Hope/Lamour, and given all that is happening, the movie felt like visiting a group of old friends. Theaters on the outskirts of Detroit don't seem as frisky as those elsewhere. Maybe it was the time or the film or the theater. However, I have noticed the behavior at a nearby square. Lots of loitering and offered rides. Strange how invisible and yet obvious it all is. Most people never see what's right in front of them. Will things ever change? Sometimes there's a mystical and almost surreal quality to living in the shadows.

Just heard the news and saw images of a horrible jet crash in Paris. Flying is a long-standing fear of mine. Once you are on the plane, you have so little control. My thoughts are with the victims and their families.

Tuesday June 5

Last night, I got good and drunk. Whiskey. I bought some during the day. When Clint came home exhausted again, I sat on the porch and had a few. The crickets were good and loud, but mixed with sirens and traffic noise. Detroit sounds different than Chicago. Last night, I was missing the Windy City. I sat listening to the night sounds and watching the lightning bugs until the bottle was empty.

Big news of the day: Catherine called Anthony to see if he would like to study Latin this summer with her. I was listening in the hall. She had me come and stand near her for support. I saw her face brighten when Anthony asked her to go see a movie instead. That was her real plan. When she hung up the phone, I congratulated her on being bold enough to telephone. "Taking initiative pays off 90 percent of the time," I told her. Laughable advice coming from me.

Catherine said I was so smart. "So, why don't you have a wife and a real job?"

The frankness of youth. I was at a loss for an explanation, so I lied. I said I had a wife, but she passed away. I said I had a real job. That I owned my own business, but the store went under. When she asked what kind of store I owned, I said menswear. I found myself excited by the lie of owning my own store and being more successful in life than I had been. In my fantasy, I'd at least tried. And even failed ownership was more impressive than working a counter at M_____. That all seemed a lifetime ago anyway.

When Catherine asked what happened to my store, I said there'd been a fire. Drama. I wanted to stop and tell her the truth, but that would've been ludicrous. For once, the truth about my life was interesting.

After a long pause, Catherine asked if I'd like to chaperone her and Anthony. I nodded and said if it was all right with her father that I would be happy to do so. Apparently, Giovanni is very strict. We're all three going to see The Phantom of the Opera with Herbert Lom tomorrow night. She's a sweet girl. I hope this Anthony fellow is nice. I've only heard about him through Catherine's bedazzled eyes. I know how deceiving that point of view can be. Love is a deforming mirror of endless enchantments.

Wednesday June 6

D-Day. Hard to believe the invasion of Normandy was eighteen years ago. A sobering thought to remember all those who were lost in the war.

On a lesser note, I also had my own battlefront. I was saddened to discover Catherine's crush, Anthony, was a jerk in the most common of ways. Had I been a youth of his own age, Anthony would've certainly been a bully. As it was, Anthony was a menace, a composite of so many fifteen-year-old boys I'd known. Cruel. Entitled. Merciless. Primal in his quest for domination. I knew his kind. A natural enemy of my kind. Those sorts of boys are eternal. The fear they spark within me never dies. They grow into people like Reginald and Nick from Housewares and Appliances. The whole lot of them stink.

Anthony was eager to expose me as a homosexual. That type enjoys being cruel because cruelty gives them an advantage. He sneered when we were introduced. I heard him whisper to Catherine that I was a pansy. She said, "What?" He leaned closer and said something I couldn't hear. An explanation, no doubt one of the basest sort. The overpowering smell of butter in the lobby was making me nauseous. Catherine turned, and I could see something had changed in the way she saw me. I was no longer an ally. I was an embarrassment. I'd received that look several times in my life, but it still cuts deeply. I'd grown fond of Catherine. She was sweet. She looked up to me. The look of disgust on her face was especially hurtful.

Anthony said, "Shall we go, Joseph?" in a lisping, mocking tone. Bowing before the seating area entrance, he added, "Ladies first." Did he think he was being clever? I hated that his family, his parish, and this society would support his behavior. I'd never done anything to purposely hurt anyone. Yet, I was the threat. I was the one who was constantly in the wrong. I was the one who needed to be on alert lest my vile nature be discovered. I hated Anthony for returning me to that shameful place. Those wounds never healed.

My head was throbbing all through The Phantom of the Opera. I sat three rows behind them. Anthony put his arm around Catherine halfway through the picture. He turned and caught my eye as he did. He was daring me to say a word. Daring me to tell him that what he was doing was wrong. Daring the pervert to censure normal adolescent behavior. To hell with them all.

Thursday June 7

A sad but unsurprising day. A predictable outcome after last night. This evening after dinner, Giovanni came up to the attic to talk to us. He looked down at his hands and said we had to leave. Clint didn't understand why and asked if he was unhappy with his work. Giovanni shook his head, "Please, you just need to go. I can't have this under my roof." Giovanni gave Clint the pay he was owed and said he wanted us out by the time he got home from work tomorrow. I asked him if I should work with Catherine tomorrow. Giovanni said Catherine was staying with an aunt and uncle. Giovanni didn't want his daughter exposed to the likes of us.

Clint couldn't make sense of Giovanni's abrupt behavior. He asked if I knew what was going on. At first I said I had no idea. A few minutes later, I told Clint the truth. He was shocked Giovanni would react that way. "What we do is no one's business but our own."

Clint is experienced, but he's very naïve in some ways. He's a different sort of invert. He doesn't understand what it's like. He can pass. Clint can fool the world if he chooses to. Many of us don't have the option. Because Clint chooses to reveal or not, he doesn't understand what it's like to have the voice and the gestures. The persona. He doesn't understand what it's like to be the revelation. I fool no one with any experience of the world. The most I can hope for is to go unnoticed, or to be tolerated and deemed a non-threat or inconsequential.

Clint doesn't expect that sort of treatment. The difference is like night and day. That undercurrent of dread needs to be felt to be understood, and once felt, it can never be forgotten. That fear has seared my brain. The dread is part of my skin, like a scar or a tattoo. My kindred brothers fear exposure. That's why we hide in big cities and aspire to invisibility. That's what made the Lawson so unique. We flocked to 30 West Chicago because we didn't need to hide or pretend to be something we weren't under that neon YMCA sign. We were allowed. Those places are rare. Clint helped me forget what that was like for a while. Clint became my sanctuary. I could be accepted and loved in his arms. In his embrace, I was worthy. Clint didn't understand that. He could sympathize, but he couldn't know. Though he held me in our attic room, I still felt isolated with the pain and sting of my demons. Those devils had arisen, as venomous as ever.

Saturday June 9

Canada is impossible without passports. If we try to cross as ourselves, we have no idea what to epxect. Clint suggested that the General has probably told immigration about us. Who knows what he may have said? Clint claims his father will stop at nothing, so I suspect we'll be promptly hauled away if we're caught. Our fates, however, will be very different. Clint will be returned home. His scandal will be hushed. As for me, Lord only knows. Committed to a madhouse? Imprisoned as a security risk? A court ordered lobotomy? Because of who and what I am, I have almost no rights.

Fake passports are the only solution. They won't be easy or cheap. Windsor seems so close (because it is) and yet so far. The Detroit River, a ribbon of water, is all that separates us from freedom. Might as well be barbed wire or lava or a bottomless chasm.

Two days have passed. We moved to a flophouse downtown. Our best bet was to find the gay underground. Someone there had to have connections. I remembered that Johnny Ray, the singer in There's No Business Like Show Business with Marilyn and Merman, had gotten busted at a place called the Brass Rail in this town for soliciting an undercover cop in the late 1950s. The address was in the phone book. 116 N. Michigan Avenue at Griswold. The place boasted the "Longest Bar in Michigan." That was someplace to start.

The bus dropped us nearby. Grand Circus Park, across the street, looked promising. Single men out for a stroll and cars circling the block. Clint always caused the cars to slow.

The wooden figures of two men drinking loomed above the entrance to the Brass Rail. We grinned at the kitschy nature of it. Most gay places don't want undue attention. The inside was dim and narrow. The bar certainly lived up to its reputation for length. The crowd didn't look gay necessarily, but it wasn't exactly an unfriendly bunch either. We made fast friends with one of the regulars, which was as easy as buying him a drink. When you're buying, the friends come fast and easy. Clint asked the guy if he knew anyone who could fix us up with something. When he gave a puzzled look, Clint said, "papers." The old guy didn't bat an eye. He didn't know anyone, but knew someone who would. He said to ask a guy named Patterson. Patterson knows everything worth knowing. "Someday that's going to get him killed," he added. Evidently Patterson hung out at the Woodward Cocktail Bar. When Clint asked where it was, the barfly laughed and said, "Woodward Avenue." We never did get the old guy's name.

The guy next to him interrupted to ask Clint if he was in the movies. Clint said no. Clint's admirer was loose with booze and clearly infatuated. "You should really be in the movies. Anybody ever told you that?" We bought them both another couple whiskey and colas and headed outside. Fresh air felt good after the smoky interior. I hadn't had a smoke in a while.

The evening was growing cooler. Fog was starting to settle. We headed west on Michigan Avenue and rounded back until we eventually found Woodward. We followed the road south a few miles to the 6426 address. Patterson wasn't around, but a cute young fellow with eyes for me said Patterson would be there tomorrow.

"Sunday nights are his thing," the young man said. When we asked where Patterson might be tonight, he shrugged. "I'm not his babysitter." The kid spun on his stool so his knee rested between my thighs. Not exactly subtle. The kid said our best bet for finding Patterson was probably the Checker Bar on Bates or the Cellar Door on Brush. But he might not be out at all. Even God rested for a day, and he's sure not Him. The young guy asked if I wanted to go somewhere and have some fun. I said I had someplace to be. "Your loss." He asked me to buy him a drink. I put down a five and told him to have a party. He said I could count on him having a good time. Clint rolled his eyes when we got outside. I told him now he knew how I felt when guys fell all over him.

We walked back to the flophouse. It reminded me a bit of Max and the Lawson. "Only a less adventurous crowd." Clint said it wasn't like the Lawson at all. The name brought back memories. "Seems so long ago," Clint said. Couldn't agree more.

In our small room, we spooned on one of the twin beds and drifted off to sleep. Tried to, anyway. Clint started rubbing up against me, his need was apparent. Oh, okay. We both needed this. I pulled off my shorts. He spit on his hand. Slow and then inside. Rocking quietly. Good as always. Moving slowly. Controlled yet urgent. The bed creaked. Slower. We didn't want trouble. Clint whispered that he loved me. Needed me. That everything would turn out fine. Having him inside me, reassuring me, calmed my fears. The apex of life. Another ideal moment. His breaths shortened. He was getting close. I whispered to do it inside me. Makes me feel so close to you. I felt the warm rush. Gasping. Grasping my hair. Wrapping an arm around my waist. Tighter. He buried his face in my back. Stifled moans.

No more chasm between us. Life and love is pure and simple again. We need to remember that all this running is really about finding. Running is about being together. Boy, if we forget that, we will never get through this.

Afterward, in the darkness. We held hands as Ray Charles's "I Can't Stop Loving You" played on the radio. "Our song," I said when it ended. Clint squeezed my hand.

We discussed the looks the man at the desk had given us. There did seem to be some suspicions on his end. We needed to find a more tolerant boarding house. All big cities have them. "There have got to be better places for us here."

Clint heard about some neighborhoods. Where I don't know. Had one of his tricks told him? Not Giovanni. Maybe a coworker. I needed to stop thinking that way.

"Maybe we should find a place in the Palmer Park Apartments," he said. "Supposedly around there, on the west side, is the place where all the artistic types live."

And we all know what artistic types is code for.

Saw in the paper today a rumor about Marilyn getting fired from Something's Got To Give. Hope it's not true. Looking forward to seeing something new from her. Not a huge Dean Martin fan. Like him better with Lewis. Alone, that guy gets on my nerves.

Sunday June 10

Despite my wish to have Clint for myself, we need cash. Fake passports won't be cheap. Hate the thought of Clint turning tricks. But I hate the thought of us getting caught or having to give up even more. Imagining him with other partners, men more attractive, men who are younger, men who are wealthier. His doing this sort of thing sparks my insecurities. Clint has no qualms about hustling. He's excited at the thought of men paying to be with him.

When Clint mentioned hustling to make us the cash, he pulled my hand to his crotch. The thought made him hard. I pulled my hand away. He kissed my neck. "What's better than being desired?"

I told him loving someone was better.

We headed to the Palmer Park Apartments. The district was gorgeous, just off Woodward and south of the park. Interesting architecture. The loveliest part of Detroit we've seen so far. No wonder the artistic types are here. When I said that to Clint, he laughed. Men were cruising him for the past several blocks. Adoration buoyed his spirits. He had an extra bounce in his step by the time we saw the sign for boarders.

I said we were father and son. The gentleman at the desk gave a look that assured me I wasn't fooling him. Clint asked if there was a shower. The desk clerk licked his lips when he looked at Clint and said there was one at the end of the hall. Made me wonder if there were peep holes carved in the wall. I signed the register as Robert Christian and Robert Christian Jr. The man joked that it was nice having Christians under the roof and asked for payment in advance. Cash. I handed him the bills. "Here you go, Dad," he said, handing me the key to our room.

When Clint asked why I chose that name, I said Christian was the only word that came to mind. Clint laughed at that. We stowed our belongings in the room. Clint had to clean up before going out. We both knew what he meant.

Clint said the Greyhound station was always a safe bet. Risky. But risks were necessary for our survival. I sat at the coffee shop across the street, had pie, and looked through the paper. Tony Bennett's debut at Carnegie Hall had been a big deal. The critics were gushing over the concert. After reading the paper, I opened Tropic of Cancer and read that for three hours. Three hours is a lot of Henry Miller. The waitress said I was going to float out of there if I had any more coffee. She said it in a nice way, but she was giving me a hint. I smoked about a half a pack of cigarettes by the time Clint joined me at the coffee shop. He winked and said we were sixty-five dollars richer. There had been no problems.

Monday June 11

Frustrated. Patterson didn't show at the Woodward last night. By the time we figured he wasn't going to show, it was too late to go to the Cellar Door or Checker Bar. Guess Sundays at the Woodward were no longer his thing. We don't have an alternative plan. That's bothersome.

Over the course of the night, Clint had a few too many drinks. Love when he gets drunk, mostly because he can't keep his hands off of me. Risky but worth it. He ravaged me in the most wonderful way when we got back to the room. Had to shush him a few times. He gets carried away. Loud. Aggressive. Unpredictable. Clint is rougher when he's been drinking. Alcohol turns him into a bit of an animal. When it comes to lovemaking, that's a good thing. I've got some bruises this morning.

Tuesday June 12

While Clint was working today, I called the hall phone at the Lawson. Not too smart. Luckily, Max was in his room. Boy, but it was great to hear his voice. He asked after us. I said things were fine. His voice dropped a bit and he said two men came around asking about us. I asked him if he said anything. He asked me if I was nuts. "I don't tell guys like that anything." Far as Max knows, no one told those bloodhounds a thing. Max said he hasn't seen them or heard word of their snooping for a couple days. He asked where we are, and I said it was best if he didn't know. Max understood. He said he misses me. The way he said it I could tell he meant as more than a friend. He was right. Max dropped hints like that now and again. Saying something without really saying something. I always pretended not to hear them. The timing was wrong with Max. The sex was good, the closeness was genuine, but I wasn't ready. I was moving in that direction, but then Clint came along and swept me off my feet. No doubt that hurt Max, but he seemed to understand.

Maybe if things were different.

Max said he hoped to see me again sometime.

I told him to take care of himself.

Double dose of Erle Stanley Gardner: The Case of the Vagabond Virgin and The Case of the Dubious Bridegroom. They pass the time. There's two more Perry Mason books on my nightstand: The Case of the Borrowed Brunette and The Case of the Golddigger's Purse. They're like eating candy, but my eyes can only focus so much on any given day. I suspect that's the result of too many dime store novels in poor light over the years.

Clint got home around ten thirty. He'd never been that late before.

Wednesday June 13

Detroit is starting to feel like a prison. The city itself isn't so bad, but I never expected we'd be here this long. Last night when I was waiting for Clint to get home, I decided to start using the cash we have. We have an okay bankroll, and we need it now. We don't need to maintain our bank if it means Clint has to keeping going with strange men, even if he wants to. We'll figure something out. We'll survive.

Patterson finally showed tonight at the Woodward. Small guy with bad teeth, crooked and rotten. His teeth, that is. Patterson must have said hello to every person who walked into the bar. Connected. After watching him a few minutes, we approached. We made small talk that we all knew wasn't small talk. Finally, Clint asked if he knew where we could get some papers. Lowering his voice, Patterson said to meet him in the bathroom. Patterson checked beneath the stall doors before asking what sort of papers we had in mind. Clint said ID. Something to get us across into Canada. Passports. Patterson said he might be able to help. I said we needed passports for both of us and started to explain our situation. Patterson held up a hand. He didn't want to know particulars.

"You give me the cash," Patterson said. "I'll be the go-between."

The passports were a thousand each. No doubt that included a healthy cut for Patterson. I couldn't blame him. He was sticking his neck out. I expected the passports to be pricey, but I had the money with me. We always carried our bankroll. I ducked into a stall and counted out twenty hundred-dollar bills. Patterson pocketed the money. He said he needed to make a quick call and dropped a dime in the pay phone. A minute later, he returned. We'd have the passports tomorrow. Patterson took us to Hudson's Department Store to get our passport snapshots. Developed on-site for your convenience. Patterson told the guy at the photo counter he'd pick up the pictures for us since we had some last minute packing to do.

Outside the store, Clint pulled Patterson aside. He got up close and said if he double-crossed us, he'd regret it. "I'll see to that personally." I liked the way Clint sounded when he said it. Tough. Sexy. Dangerous. Patterson smirked. He looked like the type who was threatened on a regular basis. Clint told Patterson we'd meet him tomorrow night at the Woodward. When we were walking home, I asked Clint where he got that line about making him regret a double-cross. "The movies," he said, laughing.

Clint and I ducked in a bar for a couple drinks to celebrate. Success! We were leaving. The night was turning muggy, and Clint was talking dirty on the way back to our room. I was anticipating some sweaty so-long-Detroit sex. When we got back to our room, the boarding house owner pulled us aside. Some plainclothesman had been snooping around about an hour ago, flashing our picture and asking questions. The old guy smiled. "I don't tell the cops nothing. Ever. Me and the police ain't on the best of terms." We thanked him and went upstairs to get our belongings. We shoved everything in our bags. We were checked out in five minutes flat.

We wondered if someone tipped them off. Maybe it was a coincidence, and they were casting a wide net. Maybe those goons were showing our picture around every decent-sized town. The General had a grudge, a compulsion to get his way, and vast resources at his disposal. Clint said nothing would surprise him.

Clint asked about getting the passports. Should we still risk it? I suspected the detectives would be staking out the gay bars. Clint suggested we get someone to pick up the passports from Patterson. Tell the guy it'll be an easy way to make twenty bucks. I liked his plan. Two grand was too much money to kiss good-bye. We headed down the street. I was suddenly dog-tired, and we needed to find a new place to sleep.

Thursday June 15

Spent Wednesday night in an all-night theater downtown. The ticket gal and counter worker didn't bat an eye when we walked in with suitcases. Probably used to it. The bus station was up the street, and the train station was right around the corner. Lots of people watching their money know it's cheaper to buy a movie ticket than to rent a hotel room.

The theater was big and cavernous with a frisky crowd and a good amount of drunks. The place reeked of marijuana. Seemed like an anything-goes kind of place. The double-bill was Invincible Gladiator and Duel of the Titans. Clint said he enjoyed those sorts of pictures. Me too. Muscles. Swords. Sweat. Codpieces… or not. I pinched Clint on the ass and said I must have a thing for bodybuilders. He shoved me back and said probably so. A blind man could have noticed the looks Clint was getting. The natives were getting restless. I suspect they were imagining him as one of the screen heroes. Steve Reeves and Gordon Scott rolled into one.

Clint threw out his chest a bit. This was getting him excited. Checked his crotch and sure enough. Hard as a rock. We took a seat. I told him to lean back. I unzipped him and went to town. The men around us moved closer, moving seats and rows at a time. Clint had his arms across the back of the seats. His hand moved to my hair. Getting close already. His hips rose from the seat. His hands moved to the back of my head. Stifled moans. His release was intense. Prolonged. I sat up, wiping my lips. He needed that. We both did. We leaned into one another and tried to get some sleep. Gladiators on the screen and a gladiator beside me.

Friday June 16

We rented a room at the Webster on the other side of town. Having investigators asking around was worrisome. I thought we had slipped by them in Rockford. We need to be on our toes and cognizant of things. We have to take steps to make ourselves less recognizable. I decided to grow a beard. At Woolworth's, I bought some hair dye and cheaters. The combination should help disguise Clint. The hair color was stinky and messy as hell. Clint claimed it was burning his scalp. He can be a baby sometimes. I told him so. Now he's a passable redhead. Thick glasses also help disguise him, though now he claims he can't see. A small price to pay. He's still sexy as hell.

Late in the afternoon, we made our way to the Woodward to see if Patterson was around. There he was. I saw him through the doorman window, sitting right between two private detectives or feds or MPs and looking awfully chummy. Either he'd ratted us out or someone said we'd been seen talking to Patterson. I had a gut feeling it was Patterson himself. I suspect a reward had been offered for information regarding our whereabouts. Cash seemed Patterson's top priority. I remembered that phone call he'd been so eager to make. Bastard!

Whether it was him or someone else, we were out two grand. And still no passports. There wasn't much we could do. Clint wanted to wait and strong-arm him. I said it wasn't worth it. They were on to us. We needed to cut our losses and disappear. Leave Detroit. Fast. From the look of things, Windsor might as well have been a thousand miles away.

Sunday June 18

They would be watching the border. Whatever the situation was with Patterson, the detectives were waiting for us to claim those passports. Kissing two grand good-bye hurt like hell.

Friday night when we got back to the room, we packed our things and headed for the bus station. The next departure was headed to Philadelphia at 10:10. The City of Brotherly Love. I liked the sound of that. Clint and I got into it during the twenty-minute wait. We'd been under a lot of pressure. Something was bound to trigger an outburst. I made a comment like, "We'd be less conspicuous if we traveled alone." I didn't mean anything by it. Just making an observation. I was right. Independently, we would be less noticeable. Maybe I wanted to give Clint an out in case he'd changed his mind. Then breaking up would be a strategy rather than a rejection. The moment I made that comment, Clint pulled away. "This is about us and being together, not about safety. If it was about safety, I'd be at boot camp and writing home to a girlfriend every day."

His outburst drew some attention. I motioned for Clint to keep his voice down. I'd never seen him so angry. He was right. This was about us. Despite his outburst, I had to smile. I was relieved he still felt so strongly about us. I apologized. His anger didn't subside until the bus was on the road for a full hour. Eventually, he took my hand in the darkness of the ride. We rocked with the sway of the bus and held hands all night. Sometimes the moments of greatest intimacy have nothing to do with sex. Silent and holding hands as we sped into the unknown was a perfect moment in the midst of all this lunacy. Clint was right. This was worth any risk. They had no right to keep us apart.

A few hours later, we arrived in Philadelphia. Neither of us knew anyone here. We'd heard Locust Street and Spruce near Quince and Carmac was the area to go. At least I recalled hearing something like that from one of the Lawson guys. Frankie? Ambrose? Sure enough, when we got there, we could tell we were in the right neighborhood. Holding stares. Single men loitering. The gay areas sometimes have a certain feel to them. That's been true of Chicago and Detroit and now Philadelphia. We found a no-frills hotel on South 13th Street. I registered us as Robert Christian and son. The desk clerk passed a key across the counter. "Looking for a little father and son time?" he said with a smile. Cheeky! I never know what to say when I'm put on the spot. I just nodded. Boy, I should've used a different name. Would the detectives recognize it? Once I realized my mistake, it was too late to change it.

We were exhausted and collapsed upon the bed.

Gorgeous full moon tonight.

Monday June 19

Exploring the city and trying to form a plan. Clint traded in his reading glasses for sunglasses. He said sightseeing was pointless otherwise. We explored and picked up some books and spent the day in Washington Square Park. Gorgeous grounds and greenery and statues. We visited the Tomb of the Unknown Revolutionary War Soldier. We both commented on the sense of history you get here. More than Chicago or Detroit. "Definitely more than Wilmette," Clint added.

Perfect day. Warm weather. We needed a relaxing day together. A day to remind us that this mad flight was worth the hardship. Doesn't seem like we should need it, but given the nature of things, we do. We need to remember it every minute. I told Clint as much in the park today. We ducked behind a tree, and he kissed me. Stupid. But worth it. No one was around. He kissed me three more times and with each peck said, "Every. Single. Minute."

Today reminded me of those lunches we shared working at M _____. The casual pleasure of one another's company. Back in the room, we practically ripped one another's clothes off. My beautiful hairy animal was hungry for me. Rough with desire. Pants pooled around our ankles, Clint bent me over the desk. After a couple spanks, took me from behind. I had him put the sunglasses on. His hands were heavy on my shoulders. He turned my head and kissed me deep. Five-o'clock shadow scratched my face. His arms encircled me, pulling me into him. His overwhelming need made the world right. He talked dirtier than ever before. Role-playing excited him. After only a few moments, he released with a whisper of I love you so much. He collapsed on top of me. The room was suddenly still. I wondered how loud we'd been. For the first time in ages, I didn't much care.

I told him it felt incredible. Best ever. Clint asked me to describe what it felt like "to be penetrated." Good was all I said. Words failed me. Clint whispered that he wanted to try. He wanted to feel what I felt when he was inside me. "I want you to fuck me, Joseph."

"Really?"

Clint nodded.

I still hadn't ejaculated, so I was ready. For the first time since we've been together, Clint allowed me to fuck his hairy ass. I loosened him up with my tongue. Then a finger. Gently. I wanted to pleasure him as never before. My arousal was greater than any I recall. When Clint was ready, I slowly entered him. I coached him to relax. Breathe into it. In. Out. Entering. Relax around it. When his breathing slowed, he squeezed my hand. A signal to begin to move. I deepened my penetration. Clint squeezed my hand. So tight and warm. Phenomenal. Yet the sensation was still overshadowed by the closeness I felt for him.

He arched his back. Greater access. He wanted more. I felt his prostate and the shivers run through him. He guided my hands to his nipples. Pull. Down and then up. With my other hand, I slapped the globes of his ass. He whispered, "Harder." I was inside the man I loved. Creating our rhythm of love. Suddenly I was so close. So near. There. Twitching and holding him tighter. Loving him so deeply. So true. We held each other through the spasms. In the midst of this embrace, my back cracked a half dozen times. We laughed at every adjustment.

We lay in silence for several minutes. Eventually, Clint grabbed the sunglasses and slipped them back on. I put my head on his shoulder. He massaged the nape of my neck. The fur of his chest was soft beneath my hand. He put a hand over mine. He kissed me and said he'd never done that before. I was his first. I asked what he thought. Clint said he liked it, but said he liked being the active partner more. He said he didn't think he could be penetrated unless he loved the person. The comment made me smile. Why wouldn't it?

I said that being the receptive partner takes getting used to. And he replied, "Then we'll have to try it again, soon."

Today was sunny and warm. We returned to Washington Square Park with books and a picnic lunch, turkey sandwiches on onion rolls and a bottle of wine that we kept in a paper bag and poured into styrofoam cups. We were still basking in the afterglow of the night before. I don't recall us talking or reading or doing much of anything. Being in one another's company was enough.

I must admit. My beard looks better than his red hair.

Around two o'clock, he slid the sunglasses down his nose and gave me that unmistakable look. We returned to the hotel, and I fucked him again. Slower. This time was not a fantasy. This time it was us. Here. Now. Joseph and Clint fucking on this day in this room in Philadelphia. Clint's moans rumbled deep within his broad chest. He was enjoying things more. This time Clint relaxed as the receptive partner. That's the key. He began to tremble. I felt the wave travel through the walls surrounding me. I felt the warmth of his ejaculate in the space between our stomachs. He reached down to get a bit of his sperm on his finger. He wiped it on his lips before kissing me.

Tuesday June 20

Our second honeymoon continues. Enchanted bliss! When we were getting ready to leave the room this morning, Clint referred to us as sexual outlaws. I like the sound of that. Fitting. Two words to capture it all.

Philadelphia is just what we needed, at least the revived closeness and intimacy we found here. The specific place is not important. In fact, we seem removed. As though we're living in a bubble. I'm unsure if this is the result of our love or our situation. Love is both our escape and our ultimate reality. Love is all that matters.

Darker reality breaks through at times, startling and violent as a stone through glass. Any stranger's stare can remind me of the peril. Why are they looking? Is it more than mere curiosity? The detectives have probably surmised we're not returning to collect our passports and we've fled Detroit. The goons are still out there. Looking. Have we made any mistakes? Left behind any clues?

Clint is still AWOL. A no-show. A criminal. A homosexual. A commie. Given the state of things and the nature of our relationship, we're both so vulnerable to the laws. No one cares about two homosexuals. They certainly don't respect any feelings we may have for one another. We're sick. Predators. A public menace. A threat to the American way of life and good citizens everywhere. We're sowing the seeds of anarchy. Locking us up is a civic duty. Ratting on us is an act of patriotism. Better dead than red. Underground what few rights we have can be easily ignored for the higher good. Who cares? We're just two queers.

Sometimes I wonder how long this running can last. Can we mold this sort of thing into our life? Can love sustain us? Some creatures live their entire lives underground. Perhaps eventually we'll just evolve. Maybe one day we'll realize we've adapted and grown accustomed to the challenges of this life. Maybe one day they won't care about us anymore.

Wednesday June 21

Technically early morning on Thursday.

The first day of summer begins on a dour note. Seeking peace of mind at three a.m. Panic woke me hours ago. I know the thrumming in my chest won't still anytime soon. Fear. Worry. Trepidation. Night Terror. Mounting panic comes with shallow breath and a heavy dread. Something is terribly wrong. This life can have no happy ending. There is no resolution to our problems. Voices say this night may be our last. Demons without substance plague my brain. Dread is nothing but smoke and vapor. A sickness of the mind. How do you quiet a shadow? Defeat a phantom? Disarm a grim notion? Nothing exists beyond this darkness.

I used to suffer these spells of anxiety every few months. Would I be arrested and jailed? Would I lose my job? Would I die in the streets? In an asylum? Would I die alone? Or behind bars? Being discovered, revealed, exposed was once the stuff of nightmares. Now discovery carries a different meaning, but a similar fear. Both rouse me in their wake. Awake and trembling.

I used to call in sick to M _____ when these shadows would descend. I called it the flu. I never took vacations. My demons ate all the time I had coming. Self-punishment. During an episode, I could only stay in my room. Wait for it to pass. Sex could take me out of my head for a bit. Then the panic would return, worse than ever.

The last time it happened Max happened to poke his head into my room. When he saw the state I was in, he climbed into bed and held me. He spent hours telling me things would be okay. He ended up calling in sick to work as well.

I thought all that had ended when I met Clint. I thought love would dispel those shadows, and it had until now. Once blind panic is gone, it's easy to forget. But when the demons return, it seems impossible they were ever forgotten. No matter how briefly. Strengthened by the night. Empowered by stressful circumstances. The fear is sharper than ever. Maybe it's only proportional to my highs. Maybe the fear is worse because there's more to lose.

Clint knows nothing of these fears. I don't plan to tell him. He wouldn't understand.

Max understood. Maybe because he was older. Maybe because he felt the same way sometimes.

Clint is asleep in the double bed across the room. I'm tempted to shake him awake and scream how desperately I need him to hold me. Like Max did. Hold me and assure me things will be all right. That I'm not alone. That I will never be alone. Just for tonight. Until these demons pass.

Clint has never seen me this way. This is not a part of me I wish to share. Even if I was tempted to express it, I won't. Neediness is not attractive. I won't let him see this weakness in me. There is no greater curse for a lover than pity. This worried man who trembles and sweats in the night is not the person that Clint fell in love with. Some burdens are best to bear alone or with a select few. Love does not wash away all our secrets, some scuttle deeper into the shadows to hide and wait.

Thursday June 22

With dawn, the demons dispersed. But now I know they're still with me. Clinging unseen. For now. Love doesn't change everything. Love is no cure-all. Love is magical, but it isn't magic. The hangover from my frantic state still lingers. Waking nightmares require recovery time. When Clint awoke, I said we needed to spend a day apart. He sat up in bed. He had questions. I said it had nothing to do with him, I just needed a day alone. Clint understood. I went to his bed. He yawned into me, stretching out like a cat over my torso. I kissed the top of his head. I could never be with someone who didn't understand the need to sometimes be alone.

He showered and dressed quickly. Ten minutes later, Clint put some of his things in a canvas bag. He kissed me good-bye and said was heading to the gym. He was eager to work out. I said I'd leave the key at the front desk and meet him back here. I handed Clint forty dollars and said to have fun.

He asked what time I'd be back, and I said seven. I told him I'd pick up something for dinner.

Clint said he might come back after working out, or maybe not.

As he headed out the door, I mouthed, "I love you."

Clint winked back and said he loved me too.

I put my journal and a few things in a satchel. I needed a reprieve from this room and the confines of my life.

I walked around Philly. Fresh air and exercise made me feel better. Eighty degrees and sunshine. I felt a slight sunburn on my face. I'm writing this in a coffee shop. Don't know what this brick and moss neighborhood is called. Philadelphia houses so much history, it seems the sun shouldn't be shining here. The brightness seems to mock all the dead revolutionaries. Life goes on. The green grass whispers Hey, forefathers, thanks. You make for great fertilizer. Even these great men are now no more than a dot on a timeline. A sobering thought. A reminder.

Time passes and we're here to enjoy life and make it count. I never understood that before Clint. My life was on hold. But things have changed. Circumstances dictate that we live in the present. We have nothing else. The future is uncertain. Next week is uncertain. Even tomorrow is a mystery. Maybe we'll be in prison or in Mexico or apart. Thinking about it is wasted energy. Being hunted is a constant reminder that all we've got is what we have now. No other moment matters.

I took the Market Street train to see more of the city. Best way to see a town is to commute through it. I was staring out the window and not thinking about much of anything when I saw the theater. So grand. I got off at the next stop without thinking. The facade was terra cotta. The marquee read Fred MacMurray and Jane Wyman. Below was written Starring in Bon Voyage! With Deborah Walley. The cornerstone of the Eureka Theatre bore the year 1913. Warm buttery popcorn, a large soda, and overlong Disney. By the time the credits rolled, all remnants of my panic hangover were gone. Maybe I didn't need a day alone as much as I needed a day in fantasyland.

After the movie, I took my time returning to the hotel. Stopped at a deli and bought our dinner. Sandwiches and potato salad. Pickles and two slices of pie. A feast. Clint was on the bed when I came through the door. I kissed him and asked about his day. He said he went to the gym and then "just hung around." I wondered if that was his way of telling or not telling me that he'd fooled around with someone. Did it matter? We lived by a different code. Conventional rules didn't apply. Living underground washed away the rules of traditional living. We had no contract or agreement. Obviously, we weren't married. If Clint did something, I didn't want to know. Some things weren't about me. Some were about needs, about libido and circumstance. He was twenty-two and attractive. Desire seemed to follow him. Who was I to deny him those isolated pleasures?

I told him I walked around and saw Bon Voyage!

"With Jane Wyman? I love her!" he gushed.

Who knew? He barely knows Garland or Dietrich and doesn't love Marilyn, but he adores Jane Wyman. Makes me worry about this younger generation. Ha-ha.

As I laid out our feast, I said we needed to discuss our next move. Clint agreed. We liked Philadelphia, but it wasn't the right place for us. We were still spooked after our narrow escape in Detroit. Time to switch towns again. We're leaving tomorrow.

After that big deli meal, we were in a semi-stupor. Soon it was time for bed. No sex on this final day in the City of Brotherly Love, just cuddling. Being in one another's arms felt wonderful. Being in Clint's arms felt ideal. Despite all the uncertainty in our lives, this was certain. This was contentment. These moments are to be savored. They are more precious than gold.

Sex had never entirely shaken the demons of panic, but cuddling could vanquish them. In some ways, cuddling is the opposite of sex. Sex is I want you and cuddling is I have you. Contentment trumps excitement in the exorcising of demons. Sleeping in one another's arms with a belly full of food was heaven after the solitary hell of last night. I slept peacefully and awoke with a smile on my face.

Clint said my beard scratches. He may be right, but it's a necessity. He said it was time for a trim. I didn't expect my beard to come in so gray. I appear somewhat scholarly. Clint called me Professor this morning. I suppose I could call him Red.

Sunday June 25

We left Philadelphia and decided to hitchhike south. I've never hitchhiked before. Clint said it was a piece of cake. He may have been the younger of the two of us, but so often, he was the more experienced.

The second person who picked us up took us quite a ways, but left us in the middle of nowhere. No explanation. Lousy luck. This is where you need to get out. I was dozing and must have missed something. He pointed us to a town just up the road, but it only had three hundred people and no motel. Folks there told us there was a bigger town just up the road. That one was sixteen miles and six hundred people. We were really in the boondocks. Then we got caught in the West Virginia rain. Thunder and lightning with plenty of wind. That was Friday. Had to wait two days for this journal to dry. The back sheets of my composition book were ruined, so I just tore out whatever pages I could salvage. I'll staple these sheets into the next notebook I buy. There are too many memories written here to throw away.

We walked half the state looking for a bed. We got stares everywhere we went. None of the three rides we got took us very far, but at least it seemed like we were getting somewhere. Who knows where you're going in West Virginia? The people were friendly enough. Strangers are not a common sight on the roads we were traveling. We finally made it to Huntington on the West Virginia River. Lovely town, but I was more thrilled to see a bus station. After a day meandering around the state, having a ticket with a set destination sounded like heaven. We ate at the diner across the street. A huge chicken and potatoes, biscuits and greens dinner for two ninety-nine. Now that was a meal! Even came with homemade apple pie for dessert.

The bus for Nashville left in the morning. Nashville was the number one travel destination for folks leaving Huntington. The ticket vendor told us so and asked if we were going to the Ralston Purina program, the Grand Ole Opry, at the Ryman. Clint lied and said yes. The man got terribly excited. He'd been there to see Kitty Wells and George Jones last year. "So close I could have reached out and touched the hem of Kitty's skirt!" He said he missed seeing Marty Robbins by a day and a half. "A day and a half! But I had to come back for work."

His comment made me sad. He felt obligated to come back to this? He'd probably been resenting it every day since. I remembered my work ethic at M_____. This guy was the way I used to be. Probably sat at his counter and dreamed of adventure. He kept talking until someone else entered the ticket line. She was going to Nashville as well. Judging by the clerk's reaction, she was not going to the Grand Ole Opry.

As we walked away, Clint whispered that he thought the ticket man was sweet. Did he feel the same way about me when he saw me behind the counter at M_____? Sweet is nice, but dismissive. I wanted to be sexy. Irresistible. Dynamic. I wanted to be the man he had to have. As if sensing this, Clint mentioned that the beard made me look dashing and capable of menace.

Nashville is green and humid, rolling and lush. Every city has its adjectives. Southern hospitality takes getting used to. That curtain of decorum comes easily. Rules of behavior are appealing. But Southern hospitality seems to disappear after a few drinks. Clint and I have witnessed more bar fights here than anywhere, and we've only been in Nashville one night. Four fights in two different bars. A Nashville benefit is the ability to get lost in the steady stream of tourists, but the town itself is too small and too expensive in the long term.

Clint let me fuck him again tonight. This time he readied himself. I went out and got Crisco and candles. This time we had a bigger bed and a door with a bolt lock. Our joining was magical, electric, and every other word that jealous people call corny. Afterward, we held each other in the candlelight.

The next morning, there were two large blobs of wax atop the wooden desk. We awoke with morning erections in need of attention. Another honeymoon phase? I could get used to this. We took turns running to the bathroom down the hall and spent the rest of the morning making love, napping, and feeling the warmth of the other. Feels so good to strip away all the drama surrounding us. Last night and this morning was us. That's what matters. The rest of this is doing what's needed to keep us together. The stress of this would make most people crumble. I don't resent Clint. I resent the situation. Why can't people let us be? We're not asking for rights, only to be ignored. I suspect most folks don't give it much thought, but those who do make up for the majority's indifference.

We just had the best fried chicken we've ever eaten, even better than Huntington. If tonight's meal is any indication, Southern cooking is a big plus for staying in the region. Maybe just not Nashville.

Monday June 26

Clint mentioned two or three times today how attractive he finds Southern men—unassuming and "fresh off the farm." Wish I could share his appreciation. When Clint talks about the beauty of others, a wall goes up. I hear the attraction as a threat. I hear They are better than you. That's not what he's saying, but my own insecurities dwarf any aesthetics. Saying something to Clint would make me sound like a fool or a prude or just plain neurotic. I've spent my life hiding my weaknesses and insecurity. Every word of praise that Clint aims at another feels like it's being somehow taken from me. He is translates into you are not. It's as if, to my way of thinking, praise comes in a limited supply. Boy, I know that sounds crazy, but I can't help it. Hate feeling this way. I have no idea how to deal with it. So I say nothing and feel the anxiety building inside me. Grow up, Joseph. Not everything is about you.

Tuesday June 27

Hard to go about life without worrying where they are and if they're nearing or disappearing. Are they giving up hope? Or tracking us with a greater determination? We're still free, but for how long? Will this go on indefinitely? I have no idea how long people will be hoodwinked by my beard and Clint's red hair and glasses. If we get caught, then what? I suspect my arrest would be handled differently than Clint's. His prison will be one without bars. A return to life in Wilmette. Coercion into marrying. Fatherhood. Normalcy. He'd be seen as the innocent led astray. I'd be labeled the corruptive influence. Someone has to be guilty. Someone always has to be at fault for all of this perversion, even if this so-called perversion is nothing more than love. Nothing more than. Ha! As though love is easy to come by.

Wednesday June 28

The good news is we got a ride out of Nashville to Chattanooga. The bad news is that it's hot as hell near the Georgia border. I only recognize the place from the Glenn Miller and His Orchestra song. Chattanooga doesn't let you forget "The Chattanooga Choo-Choo". Being here makes me wonder how people exist in this heat and humidity.

Heat makes me cranky and stupid. Clint tried to cuddle this afternoon, and I pulled away. "I love you, but no. I'm like a dog in summer. Don't touch me." Clint didn't take it well. He was short-tempered and overly sensitive. When I turned away, Clint got mad and headed out the door. He hollered that he was going to the gym. I asked him what gym, and he paused at the doorway without turning, "I don't know, I don't know this town. Chattanooga has to have a gym." When I asked when he'd be back, he said, "I'll be back when I'm back" and closed the door. I am a nag.

Strange. We know so much about each other, yet I don't know Clint's birthday. I feel bad about earlier, but I'll make it up to him when he comes home. I'll explain about the heat and my nerves. Sex always puts him in a good mood. An apology and an orgasm should make everything right. But for now, solitaire.

He's making me crazy. Bought a pack of smokes.

Thursday June 29

Now I'm the one who is mad.

Furious.

Clint didn't get back to the room until this morning. He didn't want to talk about it. I said I was worried. "Do you realize that if you don't come back, there is no one I can call. We don't know anyone here. I can't call the police. I don't know if you've been picked up or hurt or if I should go looking for you or stay here or run because they've tracked you. You could have at least called."

He wasn't interested in hearing all that. He said, "I couldn't call. I don't know the name of this place."

That quieted me down. He went into the bathroom. I took a minute and had a smoke. Smoking slows my breathing. When he came out, I was calmer. I asked where he was last night. He said he met a guy named Ned at the gym. He said it wasn't a sex thing. Nothing happened. Supposedly Ned wasn't that way. Clint called Ned a "guy's guy." He said they went and saw The Man Who Shot Liberty Valance and then hung out and had some beers. John Wayne movie. It figures. Clint said he passed out on Ned's couch. Nothing happened, he repeated. Clint said it was nice just hanging out with a normal guy. He might not have been trying to hurt my feelings, but he was succeeding. A normal guy? What the hell was that supposed to mean? Was I some sort of freak? Now I was really angry.

Clint was oblivious. He yawned and said he needed some sleep. Now I was the one heading out the door. I needed to be away from him. I was afraid of what I might say if I didn't leave that room.

Go to hell!

Later: I'm shaking my head at the lunacy of it all. I'm at a diner called Shirley's having coffee. I'm trying to stay away for a decent amount of time, otherwise he won't take my anger seriously. The fact that I'm playing this stupid game rather than lying beside the man I love makes me angry. This is all so damn childish. I'm forty-two, yet acting like an adolescent. Ego won't let me give in just yet. I have my pride. I was offended not to be considered "male company." What did that mean? So what if I'm not as masculine as he is. Despite Clint's love for me, has he always been a bit ashamed to be in my company? I was man enough to fuck him. Is that what this is about? A need to reclaim his machismo?

Half an hour. I need to disappear for longer than this. Maybe I'll go to a movie or a bar. Maybe he'll awaken and wonder where I am. Games. The older I get, the more I see that so much behavior is little more than playground antics.

Friday June 30

We made up in a wonderful way. When I got back to the room, Clint had flowers and a bottle of wine. I wanted to be mad, but what he'd done defused my anger. Clint enveloped me in his arms. I felt swallowed whole. Being consumed in that way felt wonderful. He began kissing my face and neck, "My baby. Joseph. My sweet. Shhh. I'm sorry. I'm sorry. I don't know what I'd do without you." As he kissed me, I felt myself begin to cry. I'd no idea that was bottled up inside. Clint said he was sorry if he'd hurt my feelings. He said I was all the man he wanted. All the man he needed. We lay on one of the beds, and he stroked my hair until I was asleep. Regardless of age, we all need to be the child now and again.

When I awoke a couple hours later, we had sex. Clint pushed me back on the pillow, slid down the sheets, and moved to the foot of the bed. I want to service you. Kisses at my toes. Working his way to my head. Then back down. Taking me in his mouth. Kneading his shoulders as he sucked. He knew the way I liked it. Feeling so good. Very good. Exploding.

A moment later, Clint kissed me. I tasted myself on his lips. He said he knew this constant running had been rough on me. Clint said we were a team. "Nothing can stop us." He put his head on my chest and kissed my stomach and navel. His red hair was starting to fade. Dark roots were apparent from this vantage point. In days, he'd be back to his natural shade.

"We need to dye your hair again."

"That burns."

I fingered his curls. "We need to do it."

"Whatever you think, you're the boss."

Sometimes Clint knew the right thing to say and was unafraid to say it.

"When is your birthday?" I finally said.

"January 10th."

"Mine is January 17th." Twenty years and a week apart. The thought caused me to smile. Close and at the same time distant.

Saturday July 1

Today was a nice diversion. We wandered around Chattanooga. Some terrific architecture. The public library. The red stone buildings. All of it surrounded by blue mountains. The Tennessee River running through the center of town. Every inch of Chattanooga seems lovely and quaint.

Clint opened the window this morning, took a deep breath and stretched. Every muscle seemed to pop into view. So gorgeous. He turned to me still rubbing his hands over his hairy chest. Thought he was going to start pleasuring himself. All this heat and humidity makes him frisky. But instead of wanting to mess around, Clint said he had to get outside and decided to go for a run. I went down by the river to read. He joined me later and brought a picnic lunch for us. More chicken. So lazy and wonderful. Quiet time with the man I love. We're good. All the threats to our relationship came from out there, from something other. Together there's only a feeling of happiness.

If life were different, I could fall in love with this sleepy place. Gorgeous. Leisurely. Inexpensive. Our money could go a long way in this town. Cigarettes are dirt cheap. The problem is a population of 130,000. Too small for two men together to remain invisible. That has become imperative. Invisibility has always been an issue in my life.

I grew up in Chicago, but the primary reason I remained there was because anyplace smaller frightened me. Boy, and with good reason. I'd met a dozen men at the Lawson who moved to Chicago from smaller towns because they'd been beaten, robbed, disowned, and all but run out of town for being queer. Every day a few arrived in Chicago under similar circumstances. Most are eager to just go unnoticed. Small towns can be brutal. Nothing many communities hate more than someone who is different, even if the person is one of their own. That's especially true when leaders start invoking God and patriotism and all that. That's when people become monsters and communities turn into mobs. A higher purpose allows that baser nature to come through and gives them permission to do horrible things. Hate becomes a duty. A sacred obligation. Folks turn ruthless, relentless. Dangerous. Many like me probably never make it to the big city. Who knows how many get beaten to death and buried in cornfields? Others flee into a marriage rather than flee town. Maybe this will all change one day and people will stop hating. But if it hasn't happened by now, it's not likely to happen in my lifetime.

Sunday July 2

Everyone is outdoors for the Fourth of July weekend. This crowd doesn't disguise us, it reveals us. People stare. Crowds make me nervous. So many eyes. Too much going on. They're smiling, but it's hard to determine their genuineness. Told Clint it was making me nervous, so we headed out of town and hiked in the mountains for the better part of the day. That's one thing I'll miss about this place. Chicago is so flat that anywhere with mountains seems terribly exotic.

When we were hiking, Clint and I again discussed where to go from here. Should we head south after the holiday? Mexico seemed a logical destination. The Mexican border is easier to cross than the Canadian, especially for Americans. Our money could go pretty far there. We could get jobs in a resort community like Acapulco or Puerto Vallarta. Clint said heading for Mexico might be what they expect. That's always his answer. They expect everything. Let's just try to find a decent place and stay there. Moving around is making us conspicuous. He saw my logic. But where? Miami?

During the hike, I actually broke down over all this. Frustration. Tears. There just wasn't a right answer. Would we ever feel safe? I loved Clint and wanted to be with him. I needed to focus on that. I had to trust that everything else would work out. Clint kissed me and said it would be okay. We heard a rustling and turned to see a woman watching us from the bushes up ahead. She took off running. Now I had good reason for my fears. What had she seen? What had she heard? Would she tell? Who would she tell? What would she tell? What would they do?

Time once more for us to get out of town. Independence Day indeed.

Wednesday July 5

We decided to leave in the morning. I was up late smoking and slept fitfully until dawn, fearing every sound of footsteps in the hallway, anticipating an angry mob on the street or the sight of burning crosses on the hillside. Had I seen too many movies or read too many novels? Nothing happened.

On our way out of town, we passed a paper stand. I saw the news item before Clint did. A bold-type headline on the front page. Lower left-hand corner.

General _____ Passes from Heart Ailment. Leader in Cold War Policy Dies Following a Sudden Illness.

Clint's father was dead.

I handed the man change and tucked the newspaper beneath my arm. Clint had no idea what was going on. I led him into a nearby alley. He asked what this was all about. I showed him the story. I watched him closely, unsure how he would react.

Clint was quiet for a long time, and then he said, "Is this my father? Is this true? My father died on the Fourth of July." He just kept turning the paper over. American Hero. Sudden illness. Policy Strategist. "I'm sure it was his heart," Clint finally added. "He worked himself up regularly despite warnings from his doctor."

I pointed to the headline, which mentioned heart ailment. Clint was in some sort of shock. He asked for a cigarette. He looked at me expectantly. In that moment, I felt so inadequate. I had no idea what I should do or what he needed or expected. He coughed and crushed the Marlboro underfoot after a single puff.

This news changed everything. Only Clint could decide our next move. Did he want to stick with the plan and head to Miami? Did he want to go back to Wilmette? Did all this running stop along with his father's heart? Were we safe to do as we pleased now, or at least as safe as we could be in this world? Clint said he needed to call his mother.

Thursday July 6

Everything happened so quickly. Clint called home. Constance said she needed him. When he asked how long, she began to cry. She didn't think she could manage. She was all alone. Clint couldn't say no. "Mother was crying and asking me to come." I didn't like it, but I understood. Awful to say of a woman who has just lost her husband, but I don't trust her. She cabled the tickets. We're on a plane heading back to Chicago. I somewhat expected her to send only one airplane ticket.

I hate flying.

Obviously, I was not invited to the funeral or to the family house. When we landed at O'Hare, Clint grabbed my hand and took me to the men's room. After looking beneath the stalls, he kissed me hard and held me. He said he loved me for being here. I hate circumstances. I hated being apart from the man I loved just when he needed me most. We couldn't even properly say good-bye in public.

Clint promised to rejoin me within a week. "We'll be together, and we won't need to run anymore." That sounded like heaven. I asked about his being AWOL, but he ignored the question. He wondered aloud if he was still in his father's will. "I might be coming into a good deal of money." When I asked again about being AWOL, he said it had been taken care of.

That was terrific. Did his mother tell him?

"Yes, a couple weeks ago."

He said it without thinking. I could see the regret on his face. He'd been in contact with her?

He said he'd been worried.

Two cabs pulled up. I wanted to flag the taxis on and ask Clint more questions. But everything happened so damn fast. The cabbie already had his bags. Clint shook my hand. My cabbie took my suitcase.

City?

I nodded.

I'd never been more aware of our lack of freedom as I was at that moment. Tears were in my eyes. I was so unsure and unsettled about things. So many questions. Clint gave me a look and promised to call soon.

Apart. For the first time in what seemed like forever. Clint was heading to Wilmette. I was headed back to the Lawson. Clint assured me this would be temporary. "She just needs to adjust to things. Let me talk to her. I'll explain."

He'd been in contact with her two weeks ago? Was that the first time he'd called her? Why hadn't Clint said anything? I'd made a call, too. Had I told him about calling the Lawson and talking to Max?

Speeding back to the city, back to the Lawson, returning to the site of my former life like a ghost. The Chicago skyline is so welcome. The city nears as my mind continues to wander. So exhausted. Even smoking seems an exertion. I could sleep for days but wonder if I'll sleep at all. Concerns and questions poke at me. Should I feel betrayed? Clint's parting words. "Don't try to contact me, I'll call you."

The cabbie is heading east down Chicago Avenue, across Orleans and North LaSalle, toward Dearborn. There. The Lawson, looking just the same. Postcard consistency. Stark blonde stone in the sunlight. Towering. Sturdy. Twenty-four-story formidable. The sight sparks so many memories.

A week. Nothing definite, but supposedly about a week. Clint said, "We can wait that long to be together without worry, can't we?"

I had nodded.

Did I have a choice?

Friday July 7

Death seems to be everywhere. The writer William Faulkner, whom I've tried to read a dozen times, died yesterday. Only sixty-four years old. When someone famous like that dies, I always wonder what it would be like to leave behind a legacy. I wonder who will remain to remember me, to mourn. Maybe this notebook will be my legacy. My voice across time.

No word from Clint. I got a room with no problem, two doors down from my former place. I paid for the week. Cheaper than by the day, though more expensive than the monthly rate. A week was what Clint had said. I wondered how many days comprise his idea of a week. The usual seven? So many factors: the funeral, Constance, the will.

The army is no longer an issue.

And he knew.

I'm not going to obsess.

Exciting to think our days of running might be over. That's more stress than most couples can endure, but we made it. I pray all that madness is a thing of the past.

I picked up a copy of the Chicago Daily News by the elevators. I was curious about what had been happening during my absence. General _____ was still in the headlines. Local Notable Mourned. Other than that, everything and nothing had changed. City corruption. A coming heat wave. The pending air and water show. Kupcinet spoke of visiting celebrities socializing at the Pump Room.

Also in the paper, Elizabeth Taylor and Richard Burton causing quite a fuss in Rome with their antics. Cleopatra looks to be a spectacle for more reasons than one! Though he is hardly one to talk, I can't see Eddie Fisher tolerating these sort of extramarital shenanigans for long. That one has an ego. Of course the Vatican has chimed in calling the Liz/Dick affair "erotic vagrancy." Charmed by the fact that Liz/Dick don't seem to care, I am fully behind anyone who says to blazes with convention and propriety and risks everything for love. That sort of courage deserves respect. If more people followed their heart, the world would be a happier place.

When the elevator door opened, who should be standing there but Max. Boy, but it was great to see him. He broke into a broad smile and hugged me. He's looking good. Fit and trim. The silver fox is handsome as ever. Max said he hardly recognized me with the beard. I'd forgotten all about my altered appearance. So much has changed that the beard seems the least of it. He turned around and followed me up to my room. After stowing my things, Max and I walked down to Plato's for a burger.

Max asked how things were going with Clint, and I filled him in on some of the details. He blew out a big breath. He'd heard about his father but had no idea as to the rest of it. Max asked if I still loved Clint.

Yes.

And then asked if we were monogamous. I laughed and said we never were. After all, we aren't heterosexuals. Walking back to the Lawson, I wondered if Max wanted to keep me company while I waited for Clint. I guessed yes. After all, we did have a past and he sure seemed to like my beard. That question regarding monogamy seemed a hint at his intentions. By the time we returned to the Lawson, I was exhausted.

Still no word from Clint.

Saturday July 8

I awoke in a panic. Dread. Fear. Then realized I wasn't running anymore. I heard men passing in the hallway. Saturday. Things sound busy. Walking the halls, the Saturday cruise. Some called it "weekend shopping." I remembered the eagerness and the loneliness I used to feel walking these halls. The desperation. The anticipation. The thrill. The inevitable comedown. I connected plenty of times with plenty of men. Finding someone often came with a rush of belonging. That feeling passed quickly. But in a few days or sometimes a few hours, the hunger grew again and again and again. There was only a brief satisfaction before something inside wanted more. It was a cycle that went nowhere.

Hung around the Lawson all day. Feared missing Clint's call. Max came by my room about noon. He was going out for lunch and asked if I wanted to go. Said I'd better wait around in case Clint called. There was a quiver in my voice when I said Clint's name. Longing or uncertainty? Max probably heard it but didn't comment. I asked Max to pick me up a sandwich. Fell asleep and awoke a hour later. Max was at the door with a ham and swiss on rye and a six pack of Falstaff. He hung around, and we did more catching up. He'd been going to the bars more since his beating at North Avenue Beach. He liked the places around Clark and Division—Jamie's, Shoreline 7, the Gold Coast.

"You've got to go with me sometime. Drinks are cheap. Frankie works at Jamie's, and he usually gives me my cocktails two for one."

Said I'd be happy to go to the bars with him sometime, but refrained from specifics. He pushed the issue. "How about tonight? I'm going over there when the restaurant closes." Max was still a waiter at the Silver Chalice. I passed. Still worried Clint might call and I won't get the message. Max said to suit myself. The way he said it made it clear he thought I was being a sap. Or maybe his feelings were just hurt. But Max didn't understand the way it was with Clint and me, and the depth of what we felt. He didn't know all we'd been through. Without Clint, I was nothing. Clint was worth any sacrifice. Waiting for a phone call was small potatoes.

Instead, Max and I decided to see a movie tomorrow. A cool theater sounded grand. The Lawson was already sticky. Tomorrow is supposed to be a real scorcher.

Sunday July 9

No word from Clint. Supposed to see a movie with Max today. Decided to hang around the Lawson just in case. Told Max I'd take a rain check. Boy but his disappointment was apparent. He rolled his eyes. None too pleased. Walked down to the Walgreens and bought a carton of cigarettes along with the thickest books I could find—Dr. Zhivago and The Once and Future King. Those should keep me busy for a while. Frankie popped his head in a couple hours later to say hello. He saw The Once and Future King on the desk and said he had heard rumors that T.H. White was a nancy! When I asked Frankie where he heard that, he said someone at the bar was talking about it. Don't know how reliable that is. Who knows?

Headache from reading or maybe smoking too much. Dr. Zhivago is good, but my eyes are lousy. About halfway through. No word from Clint.

Monday July 10

The Lawson feels like home: the sights, the sounds, the smells. The men. But I can only sit around here so long. Then it becomes a prison. Max came by the room around noon. He was taking me out and wouldn't take no for an answer. He grabbed my arm until I started laughing and said, "Okay, okay." I said to give me a few minutes to get dressed. Max said he didn't need to leave. He looked at my crotch and said he'd seen it all before. Wouldn't mind seeing it again. I laughed off his come-on. Nothing happened, but part of me wanted it to. After all, Max and I understood one another awfully well.

Max and I had sandwiches at Goodwin's Deli on Wabash. Such fun to sit and talk and watch people walking by. The world passes by those front windows! After lunch, we headed across the river for a double-feature. Madison Avenue with Dana Andrews, Jeanne Crain, and Eleanor Parker—a big soap opera set against a backdrop of the advertising industry. Kind of a bore, but a glossy one. Madison Avenue was on a double-bill with the much more entertaining House of Women starring Shirley Knight. Max and I giggled through much of the picture. He's so much fun to be with. I'd forgotten how good it feels to be silly. Plenty of action in the balcony during this double-feature. I didn't participate. Neither did Max. We laughed that the theaters near the bus terminal never disappoint a lonely gentleman. Nice to socialize with someone closer to my age. Someone simpatico. Clint's youth is refreshing, but the twenty years between us can stretch awfully wide sometimes.

After the show, Max asked me if I wanted to go work out when we got back to the Lawson. Since I hadn't heard from Clint as of yet, I said sure.

Walking back to the Lawson, who should we see but Nick from M_____, one of the Housewares and Appliances assholes. He looked right at me but didn't say a word. After we passed him, I turned to Max and mentioned I knew that guy and he just walked by.

Max shrugged. "You did the same thing." Couldn't argue with that. Max said maybe he didn't recognize me with the beard. Never considered that. I asked Max, "Do I really look so different?" Max thought for a moment. He said it wasn't so much the beard, but I just carried myself differently. When I asked what he meant, Max said I had an added confidence. Max said he liked it. He called it sexy. Max is so cute sometimes.

When we returned, we changed and met each other in the gym. Exercising felt good. We did the stationary bicycles and some sit-ups and calisthenics before taking a long steam. Found myself even more attracted to Max than I'd been earlier in the day. In the haze of the steam room, I wished Max would reach for me. I wouldn't have stopped him. I didn't know how to let him know without seeming full of myself. I loved Clint, but I wanted Max. Badly. I needed affection and attention. Later, I tried and failed to sound casual when I reminded Max that Clint and I were a couple, but not exclusive. "He has his dalliances and I have mine."

Max and I had messed around plenty before. Even done more than messed around. We were good together. But it was never serious. Timing. Neither one of us was ready. What we had was never more than attraction and friendship… which suddenly seems like a great deal. What more can you hope for really? Though Max seems to like my beard, I plan on shaving tomorrow. Can't have folks thinking I've become a long-in-the-tooth beatnik.

Went to the TV room and watched The Danny Thomas Show and then Andy Griffith. There was a big to-do because some fellows were Troy Donohue fans and wanted to flip the channel and watch Surfside 6. A well-built negro across the room was making eyes at me during the ruckus. I thought I was misinterpreting at first, but no. He followed me upstairs and overtook me at my door. His voice was deep and his gaze intense. He introduced himself as Ryan. A formal handshake. Ryan asked if I wanted to talk for a while. He took a step closer. Get to know each other. I knew what that meant. Such a beautiful man. I told him I had someone. He said he did too, and winked. That made me laugh. Ryan said, "Raincheck" with a smile. Ryan is staying right down the hall in my old room. What a wild coincidence!

Such a full day, even without Clint. I feel so desirable! Maybe I won't shave the beard. Who knew a beard and some confidence could change everything? I lay down on the bed and had a smoke and thought about Clint. I ended up pleasuring myself, Clint became Max at times and Max became Ryan at times. Clint and I needed to reconnect. I felt adrift in a sea of lifeboats.

Stayed up late reading Dr. Zhivago. Reading a novel set in such turbulent times makes my problems pale in comparison. A distant lover. Too many suitors. Maybe life is always a matter of attitude and perspective. Someone always has to have it worse. That doesn't change the circumstances, but hopefully opens the door for gratitude. I miss Clint, but Max and Ryan are welcome distractions. The most frustrating thing is the uncertainty. I've always had a need to be so sure of where I stand and what is what. Maybe current circumstances are an indication I need to amend that. Most times the world doesn't give a damn about my plans, and God cares even less.

Already sore from working out. The kid who moved in next door is a folk singer, but his playing isn't too disruptive as of yet. Just a guitar and his warbling. Soothing, really. The way he starts and stops, he must be writing songs. Most are about social justice. Peace. Love. Brotherhood.

Good night!

Tuesday July 11

Clint called today!

Luckily, I was in my room when the phone at the end of the hall rang. I answered it myself. No time lost tracking me down. Clint was surprised when I answered. "Joseph?" He asked what was new. I said nothing. The Lawson was much as we'd left it. Told him Max said hello. I said I'd been waiting for his call. Clint said he liked to hear me say that, and he apologized for not phoning earlier. Constance still couldn't be alone. She was napping at the moment. Thursday, he was taking her to a doctor in Evanston for treatment of a possible nervous breakdown. He said she really needed him now. More than ever. I felt like answering that I did too. Instead, I said I understood. Sometimes being understanding is a curse. Often it means other people's needs come first. That makes me resentful. I asked Clint when I would see him again. He promised to call Thursday night. I asked for his number in case I needed to reach him. He didn't think that was such a good idea.

When he said it, I was so mad I wanted to hang up. A dial tone would be more eloquent than I was capable of being at that moment. I felt like saying maybe I was just too dirty of a secret to even have! Why shouldn't I call? Constance already knew about us. She was already having a nervous breakdown. How much damage could a call from me possibly do? My patience was running low. Clint must have sensed my anger. Boy, steam was probably rising from the receiver on his end.

Clint said if I just waited a few more days, he would make it up to me. He promised things would be different once the estate was settled. We'd have all the money we needed and wouldn't have to run anymore. I said I didn't care about the money, but I don't think Clint heard me. Just then he covered the receiver and said something to someone in the room. I suspected Constance had awakened. Maybe he was talking to a relative or domestic. I didn't know much about his life in Wilmette, other than they were quite wealthy. Clint said he had to go. He would call me Thursday evening after seven. I said okay, and I added I love you. Clint had already hung up. Rather than getting answers, the conversation left me with more questions.

Now what?

The conversation was upsetting. Max was downstairs. Ryan was down the hall. I looked at myself in the mirror on the back of the door.

I am keeping the beard.

Wednesday July 12

Ryan was in the bathroom area this morning when I went to wash up. He said hello and gave me the eye, and then he dropped his towel and headed to the showers. He was a gorgeous ebony statue. Endowed. And clearly he wanted me to know about that. Why would a man like that want anything to do with me? I brushed my teeth and washed my face. Leisurely. Distracted by the spray of the shower. Perhaps I was dawdling a bit. Waiting. Ryan emerged from the spray and toweled off. Larger. His manhood was swollen. Floating. He caught me staring at him in the reflection of the glass. He draped the towel over his shoulders and approached. He stood behind me, held my gaze in the mirror. I could feel his heat. Ryan flashed a smile. "Big plans for today?" I shrugged and said nothing in particular. "Oh really?" His smile got bigger as did certain parts of his anatomy. I'm blushing even as I write this.

We had a grand time back in Ryan's room. So happy to lose myself in pleasure and not worry about Clint or anything. Ryan was wise to things. Getting together with a buddy at the Lawson meant nothing, just two guys helping each other out. I reminded him I had a boyfriend, and he reminded me that he had one as well. Ryan said my boyfriend must be a very lucky guy. My sudden appeal still baffles me. Ryan asked about Clint. I gave him an abridged version of what was going on. He asked more questions. Maybe he was nervous. I finally said, "Enough!" Or maybe Ryan was just being overly polite.

My love life could not possibly interest him. Ryan kissed me hard. "Maybe Clint doesn't appreciate you the way a man should?" I said he was good to me. Ryan began to rub his body on top of mine. "This good?" he said. I didn't get back to my own room until after dinner.

Max came by to see if I wanted to hang out and saw me leaving Ryan's room. I was sure I must have been wearing a big smile. Max pulled me in my room and asked what I knew about Ryan. I said I didn't know anything. "He's just a buddy." Max knew what I meant by that. My smile revealed everything.

Max told me Ryan had been asking about me before I returned to the Lawson. He said Ryan moved into my old room a couple weeks before I returned. He said he didn't think it had been a coincidence. He requested that room. Max added that he thought Ryan had been one of the guys asking questions after Clint and I disappeared. I asked if he was sure. Max said he wasn't positive, but I should be careful. Ryan was hitting on me awfully hard. A guy like that could have anybody. An ulterior motive made a lot of sense. I wondered what that motive might be. Max asked if I told Ryan anything. Not really. Nothing important. I remembered discussing my situation, and his questions, but in the aftermath of passion, I couldn't remember exactly what I'd told him or how detailed I'd been.

Max asked if I wanted to go get something to eat. That sounded good. I had to get out of this place and try to make sense of things. As we were leaving the Lawson, we saw Ryan a couple of|blocks ahead, walking west on Chicago Avenue. A moment later, he headed down the subway stairs. I wanted to turn away, but Max said we should follow him. "Don't you want to know what this is all about?" I nodded yes, but I had my doubts. I was afraid of what I might discover. Sometimes ignorance is bliss. I wanted life to be boring again.

Thursday July 13

We lost Ryan in the underground. Max and I were in the car behind him. We could see him, but the cars got crowded. When the train pulled out of Randolph Station, he was gone. Maybe he got out there or switched cars. Far as I knew he hadn't seen us. Max and I ate at Italian Village. So good. And always such fun to get one of the villa-like booths. Our dinner felt like a date. I wondered if that was the result of the energy between us or the situation happening around us. Maybe it was a combination of the two.

Max said that at least Ryan didn't know I knew about him, and it was probably wise to keep it that way. "You'll learn more by being friendly." Max was right. Yet part of me didn't want to learn more. Ignorance had been such bliss. Now I knew just enough to snatch that contentment away.

Spent the morning wondering about things. Theories. Reasons. Spinning my wheels with possibility after possibility. Such a futile way to spend a part of the day. But in reality I have nothing but time.

Ryan knocked on my door and asked if I wanted to get some lunch. Max was right. The best way to learn more was by interacting with Ryan. I told him sure and said I'd be a minute. Ryan came in and closed the door. He adjusted himself and said he liked watching me dress… and undress. I told Ryan if we started anything, we'd never eat.

"Not food anyway," he said with a grin.

At the corner deli, he asked what I had planned for the day. Clint was supposed to call, but I said nothing except I had a commitment for the evening. Ryan made a sad face. Time to do some prying of my own. I asked where he was from. The suburbs. I asked where he worked. An office downtown. I asked which one. He said a place on Wacker. He was in sales and mentioned something about financial markets. I mentioned his hours seemed pretty leisurely. He claims he recently switched positions. His new job didn't start for another week. Everything was vague. Evasive. And yet, perfectly plausible. Most queers aren't too keen on sharing specifics. That was how jobs were lost and lives got ruined. I eased the questioning. Didn't want to make him suspicious.

Clint called about nine thirty. I was about ready to give up when the hall phone rang. He sounded exasperated. The line had been busy for an hour. I said that's why it might be easier to have his number. Clint said nothing. He still seemed pissed off. His mother needed more time. The doctors said loss was always difficult. She'd had a terrible shock when she discovered her husband dead in the bed beside her. The MDs were hopeful for her complete recovery. He had no idea how long that might take. I asked when he could visit. He couldn't really leave his mother alone. She needs me. I shot back, I need you! I cringed at the needy tone in my voice.

Clint didn't like the situation any more than I did. He claimed he didn't mean to sound short, but things were tense at home. I said I knew a way to calm him down. He laughed. That was so welcome. Laughter made him sound like the old Clint. He said he needs me. The words warmed my heart. Needs. That simple declaration pushed all my doubts and concerns aside. He'd see what he could do about coming into the city for a day. I told him that would be wonderful. I said I loved him. This time he said he loved me, too.

When I hung up, I turned. Ryan was standing at the doorway to his room. He asked me if I wanted to come talk. I knew what that meant. In case I was unsure, he groped his crotch to clarify. I said I wasn't feeling well. He asked if there was anything he could do. I said I just needed a good night's sleep. "Maybe tomorrow," he said, closing his door.

Back in my room, I lay on the bed and forgot I still had to brush my teeth. I headed to the bathroom. At the end of the hall, I noticed Ryan. Despite two other open phones, Ryan was at the pay phone I'd been using. He didn't appear to be calling anyone. Seeing me, he smiled. That gorgeous grin was supposed to mask intent and make me forget everything. Ryan hit the receiver and said the phone was giving feedback. Moving to another phone, he began to dial. Hope I didn't appear too suspicious. I ducked into the bathroom. I locked myself in a stall. This is insanity. I don't know what to believe.

With the General dead, why should any of this matter? Unless the General wasn't behind having Clint and I followed. Maybe the General wasn't the relentless one after all.

Friday July 14

Max came by this morning to see what I was doing. I told him about Clint's phone call and Ryan's subsequent behavior. Max repeated that I needed to keep acting like I didn't suspect a thing. "You'll be safer that way." Safer?

I said I didn't think I could handle it today. Max suggested we spend the day together. I'll take your mind off of things. Good idea. I wondered if Max had ulterior motives. The thought of spending the day with him made me smile. He knew how to turn my mood around. Max said he'd meet me downstairs in an hour.

Ten minutes later, Ryan came by and asked what I was up to. Said I'd completely forgotten I'd promised Max we'd do something today. Ryan kissed me. He was so handsome with such appeal. Ryan made it so easy to pretend to be infatuated. Yes, I was that shallow sometimes. Why shouldn't I be? His body felt wonderful. His muscles and his manhood pressed against me. I felt a stirring in my slacks. He slapped my ass and growled that tomorrow he had me all day. Told Max all about it over lunch. He threw a bone just hearing about it secondhand.

We walked over the river and saw Experiment in Terror with Glenn Ford and Lee Remick. Terrific movie, but it didn't take my mind off everything going on at the Lawson. I'd gone from leading a boring life to leading one of intrigue. Careful what you wish for. No middle ground. When we got back, Max said he'd meet me at the pool. Said he had plans for us and winked. So comfortable being with Max. The timing was wrong before, but maybe not anymore. Uh-oh.

After our swim, I expected some fooling around. By then I was ready. Nope. Instead, Max said he was taking me out on the town. I told him I didn't enjoy the bars. He made a face and said maybe I'd just been to the wrong places. "Besides," he said, "you need to unwind a bit."

Max is right, and even when he's not he is very persuasive.

Saturday July 15

Where does the unwinding end and the bender begin? My head is still pounding. I'll capture what I can remember. Almost three in the afternoon, and I've just managed to brush my teeth. Even that was painful.

Had no idea there were so many gay places in Chicago. I'd heard about the bars and even wandered into a couple of them. I went to the Lincoln Baths a couple times on North Clark, but that place depressed me. Low ceilings. Crumbling walls. Desperate-looking clientele. I came, and then I went. I had better luck at the Lawson.

Max said the bars had come a long way. He said a lot of powerful people knew good money was to be made off the pansies. "We drink like fish, you know," Max had joked. He said that the queer bars had protection now. A place wouldn't be raided unless someone wasn't getting their money. Max said he's seen the doorman at a couple gay bars run right out with a paper bag of cash and give it to some guy in a fancy car. When they didn't get that money, things didn't go so well. Max said that's what had happened with the Shoreline 7 raid last week. He added that the rules tended to change around election time. "Vice raids and a crackdown on perverts are always a popular political stand."

Max has to be extra careful. He's been nabbed before in a pervert sweep. That's why he worked as a waiter instead of a teacher. Can't have queers around kids. The arrest was why his wife threw him out. She told their son that Max had died. Better that than telling the lad the shameful truth. Having his name in the paper, and the aftermath, cut Max to the core. Everything, gone. One more bust, and they'd send him away. For an indeterminate period. We've all heard what happens to our kind in prison.

We started out at the Front Page on Rush Street. Odd place. Regular bar upstairs and a gay bar in the basement. Smoky as hell down there with no ventilation. Not many fellows lining the stools, but Max knew the bartender. Two fellows leaning against the bar had just gotten back from New York. They'd seen How to Succeed in Business Without Really Trying and were raving about the show. Max didn't believe me when I said I'd never seen a Broadway show. I've never even been to New York.

What! No one could believe it.

Two other men came in that Max knew. Then another. I told Max he seemed to know a lot of people. He said waiting tables was a great way to meet fairies. He claims half the restaurant workers downtown are queers. We had a few drinks and met a guy named Mort who was both Lana Turner's and Yvonne DeCarlo's driver when they had shows in town. He had some great stories. When we left, he slipped me his phone number. Forgot all about him until this morning when I found the matchbook with his number in my pocket. Life really does begin at forty. Or in my case, forty-two.

Next we headed to Jamie's at Clark and Division. Even though I'm naive about this sort of thing, that bar has the feel of a mob operation. The back office. Guarded. The muscle at either end of the bar. Frankie said the mob picks the jukebox company and the beer distributor. Even down to the towels we use. He said to keep my mouth shut about it, though. From the looks of

Jamie's, the mob also had a vested interest in the hustler trade. The rent boys hung around the pool tables and the cigarette machine. Frankie was bartending. He gave us a couple free cocktails. The clientele called him Doris. The jukebox was playing Dion's "The Wanderer" and "Spanish Harlem" by Ben E. King. I only remember because it played both songs three times in a row! Frankie camped it up here even more than at the Lawson. Stuck a plastic flower in his hair when "Spanish Harlem" came on. He's so funny. When we stumbled out the door, Max said we had one more stop.

Next door was the Gold Coast. I'd heard this was a biker bar, but I had no idea what that meant. I figured greasers and would-be Brando and James Dean types. When we opened the door, a guy started asking if we knew what kind of bar this was. Asked me if I used cologne. Max put an arm around me and said I was okay. Once we passed the doorman, we rounded a curtain and went inside. The place was made to look like a back alley. The murals on the wall were of muscled men in dungarees and dark alley scenes with guys looking for action. Like someone had torn a page out of my secret fantasies. How did the artist know? My eyes must've about bugged out of my head. When we ordered beers, the bartender said he liked my beard. Said he'd like the feel of it tickling his thighs. I blushed, but boy I sure liked the directness. Men here were that way. The place was charged with sex. Electric with it. Max said it was always jumping on Friday nights. After an hour, we headed back to the Lawson.

Max spent the night in my room. Cozy. I love the smell of him. We played around a bit, but nothing really happened. Not for lack of trying, too drunk. Both happy not to feel so alone. We needed each other. Heard a knocking on my door a few times earlier. Probably Ryan. Max went back to his room around noon.

He has to work later today. Hope he isn't as hungover as I am.

Went for a steam downstairs around six. Needed to sweat out some of this alcohol. Ryan was there. Asked how I was doing. I gave a look that said, "shoot me now." He said it looked like I had fun last night. He asked if I'd seen my boyfriend. I said no. Ryan heard Max and I come in around two. Was he waiting for us? Ryan said we sounded happy. He reached over and grabbed me. His touch was electric. He pulled me against his muscled body and began kissing me. My mouth. My ears. My throat. Even if I wanted to resist, I couldn't have. He stroked me to release and licked his fingers clean. Asked me to spend the night with him. I declined. I needed to sleep. He said we could do that. We don't have to mess around, we can just talk. He's expecting me in his room in ten minutes.

Sunday July 16

Clint called. He's coming to town Tuesday and staying downtown until Thursday morning. So excited to see him again. Things have been crazy with Ryan and Max and being back at the Lawson. Almost forgot what all this was for. Almost. Funny how short my attention span can be when I'm thinking with other parts of my anatomy. I hope Clint has some answers for me.

Monday July 17

Ryan came by the room after I talked with Clint yesterday. He wanted to know if I had plans. We went out for lunch. So strange. We were having burgers, and people were giving us looks like we were from the moon because Ryan is colored and I'm white. I can only imagine what they would think if they knew we were mixed-race queers. They'd probably have us killed before boiling the dishes. Ryan hardly noticed. Finally, I said something. He said, "Welcome to my world." He gets that sort of thing all the time. Stares. People double-checking their wallets. Pulling children closer. Crossing the street when they see him coming. Women figuring him for a rapist. He said he didn't know how long things would go on. He claimed something is going to happen. Ryan said a lot of Black folks out there were frustrated and angry. Bubbling over. He said they weren't going to tolerate this sort of treatment forever. It's even worse in the South. When I asked when he'd been there, he changed the subject.

I told Ryan my boyfriend was coming into town tomorrow, and he started to get real curious. How long was he going to stay? Would he be staying at the Lawson? Why wasn't I with him all the time? What were we going to do? I talked about it a little but avoided specifics. Wasn't sure if I did the right thing bringing it up, but not mentioning it would be suspicious. When I asked Ryan about his boyfriend, he said he was in the service. Interesting.

Ryan asked if I wanted to mess around, but I said I wanted to be ready for Clint. He asked me what Clint and I liked to do. Trying to make a joke of his asking, I said none of his beeswax. Strange he'd ask that.

Went to the gym tonight and hit the TV room, but they were watching Bonanza. No thank you! Thankfully it was almost over. Candid Camera was a scream.

Full golden moon tonight. The kind of moon that begs for baying hounds. Clint arrives tomorrow!

Tuesday July 18

Just got a call from Clint. He's staying at the Stevens Hotel on South Michigan Avenue. Fancy. He said to pack a bag and come to the hotel after noon. He said I could stay with him there for the next couple of days. I asked what room, but he said he hadn't checked in yet. Clint said he'd meet me in the lobby.

Thursday July 20

A whirlwind couple of days.

The Stevens is so grand. The ceilings, the chandeliers, the staircases. All the evidence that it was once the place to be, though in recent years it's fallen into disrepair. Clint met me in the lobby. I was reading A Burnt-Out Case by Graham Greene. Okay. Not one of my favorites of his. Clint nodded for me to follow. I was unsure if he was being discreet because of the locale or because of our personal intrigue. When we got to room 1002, he practically ripped my clothes off before he stripped down. My man was ready to go. Muscled, hairy, erect, and wearing a hungry grin on his face. He flipped off the lights and tackled me on the bed. He took me roughly the first time. Merciless and so good. Without stopping, he went again. Have I sung the praises of youthful stamina recently? It bears repeating.

After we lay sweaty and spent upon the sheets. I told him about Ryan seeking me out after he'd presumably been asking questions about us weeks before. Clint asked what he looked like. Something seemed to click when I told him, but he said it was nothing. I said Ryan was still digging for information, but I didn't understand why with the General dead. Clint said he had no idea. I think he did. I asked if he was sure. He said a man named Preston had been using similar tactics in Wilmette. They'd met at the gym. Great sex. Subtle questioning. He said he was baffled as to their motives.

I wonder what they're after.

I put my head on Clint's hairy chest. Despite the tense circumstances, it felt so wonderful to hear his beating heart. "If it isn't us in particular, then it must be something we know." Clint toyed with my hair. "Or have." I said Ryan didn't seem to be looking for anything in particular, though he is staying in my old room. I said Ryan's questions weren't very pointed. He was just overly curious. Clint said maybe they weren't sure what they're looking for. Clint also suspected his home phone line was bugged.

Nothing was clearer, but it was interesting to know this Preston and Ryan were both using the same sort of sexual espionage. Apparently Ryan and Preston and their boss didn't expect Clint and I to discuss our sideline dalliances. They didn't know the connection we had.

We ordered room service and ate dinner in our robes. Then sex again. Clint seemed starved. I joked with him that Preston must be lax at his job. Around ten, we went for a walk. The night was perfect, in the seventies with a nice breeze off the lake. The moon looked as full as the night before. I told Clint that Max had taken me to some bars. Clint asked if I wanted to go to some. I said not tonight. Tonight I want you all to myself. If we went anywhere, the guys would be on him like flies. He grinned in a way that showed off his dimples. He liked the idea of guys finding him irresistible. Not sure if that meant he had a healthy or an unhealthy ego. I told him guys were liking my beard. He said it looked good on me, but I needed a trim.

We stopped at an out of the way place and had a couple beers. A booth. Clint was even more handsome in the candlelight. "The Theme from A Summer Place" was on the jukebox. Looking into Clint's eyes was paradise. I'd missed him so much. The moment would have been perfect if I could have touched him, but I knew what that would mean. Neither one of us wanted to go to jail. I envied the couples freely holding hands all around us. Did they appreciate their freedom? Did they have any idea what it might be like to have their love be an issue? I could only be bitter for so long. I was so fortunate. The way Clint was eyeing me, I knew what was coming when we got back to the hotel. I was right. We didn't even make it to the bed.

Woke up about seven. The ghost of the moon was near the horizon. Beside me, Clint was sleeping on his stomach and lightly snoring. His hairy muscular butt looked so great in the morning light. Two perfect globes. Firm and furry. I leaned down and lay my cheek on them. I kissed one and then the other. Clint began to stir. Rocking his hips. He looked over his shoulder and grinned. "Good morning," I said.

"Best way to wake up," he said, reaching back to pull my face into the crack of his ass.

After making love, we napped again and got out of bed a couple hours later. We made it down to the lobby around noon. We had coffee and read the newspapers. Loved the complimentary cigarettes in the crystal holders on the side tables. Clint looked at me lighting a smoke. "I thought you had quit, or at least cut down."

"Me too," I said with a shrug. If anything I'd been smoking more.

I brought my journal and told Clint I had to write this down. There was a piece in the paper about this guy named Andy Warhol who had an exhibit featuring paintings of thirty-two Campbell's soup cans. The world is going mad. I showed the picture to Clint. He couldn't believe it either. We both laughed that we had been eating art for years without even knowing it.

Twentieth Century Fox dumped Jayne Mansfield. Or rather, opted not to renew her contract. About time. Never cared for her. Imitations strike me as sad, and Mansfield always seemed to be trying to out-Marilyn Marilyn without understanding what she is about. Marilyn has a softness and an innocence. Take away those elements and add crudity and you have Mansfield. The story went on to say Mansfield was ecstatic about the studio contract ending and about feeling free. I'll bet. When I showed that piece to Clint, he just shrugged. He indulges me, but he isn't one for star gossip.

I had smoked a bit too much. By the time we headed out for lunch, my throat was sore. When I mentioned it to Clint, he said it sounded like my throat needed to be coated. He had a one-track mind. I loved it. I must have looked over at him a dozen times that day and thought, God, I love this man. How had I endured our time apart? Any doubts I had about us vanished in the brilliance of being back together. My only fear was that he didn't feel the same way. What fellow wouldn't be insecure in my shoes?

We left the hotel and headed north on Michigan Avenue. Who should I see a few feet ahead of us but Ryan? I pulled Clint into a doorway. "That's him. That's Ryan. The black man in the khakis and plaid shirt a half block ahead."

Clint stuck his head out. "Let's follow him."

Against my better judgment, I agreed. We moved into the flow of pedestrian traffic. Clint put on his sunglasses and told me to keep my head down. Ryan went west on Monroe and turned again on Wabash before crossing. Ryan ducked into a building along the elevated train tracks. The rooms were above a jewelry store. We looked at the register downstairs. A couple offices with just names: C. Kline, F.A. Schwieger, P. Willingham. Also a place called Passport Photo Express. As we were looking at the register, we heard the outside door shake, as though someone had entered one of the office doors upstairs.

"We can wait," said Clint.

"And do what?"

Clint looked angry. "I want to find out what the hell this is all about."

I didn't think it was safe and told him so. "We don't know what or who we are up against. They could even be watching out the office windows. He might've even known we were trailing him. He's not stupid. I doubt it was much of a coincidence he happened to be strolling near our hotel."

Clint knew I was right.

"We have to be patient."

I bought a pack of cigarettes. We had more coffee. I asked Clint if he was sure his father hadn't told him anything. Maybe he had overheard something. He said he heard the General on the phone all the time. "He hated closing his office door. He'd been captured and tortured by the Japanese during WWII. Closed doors made him claustrophobic."

"Are you certain?"

Clint didn't recall anything in particular. "But..." He said he did recall his father meeting with some men on the trip to Paris. The General said he needed to be alone for a business meeting, so Clint and his mother had left the room. They were a few blocks away when Clint realized he'd forgotten his wallet. "I ran back to the room and entered without knocking. My father was there with several men. They look startled to see me, and the guards drew guns." I asked Clint if he remembered them. He didn't. Nor could he quite remember what they were talking about. "Something about farming. Like I said, it was only for a second, but Father's expression told me it was something big. They stopped talking as soon as they saw me. I got my wallet and figured that was the end of it. He never mentioned it to me again, and I never brought it up."

I had no idea what to make of this Paris incident. Maybe this was nothing. I hadn't told Clint, but I thought Constance was behind it all along. She never told the General. And Ryan and Preston were simply her latest attempt to sabotage our relationship. New lovers and sparking jealousy were the oldest tricks in the book. Maybe Clint's homosexuality wasn't what bothered her. Maybe his loving another person was the real threat. Maybe she realized that when he wanted to leave Paris early.

We saw The Notorious Landlady with Kim Novak and Jack Lemmon. Afterward, Clint treated me to a steak dinner, and then we walked around the Loop. There seemed to be a folk singer or a duo on every other corner. Some are good. Some not so good. When we got back to the Stevens, Clint paid for a proper trim for me at the hotel barbershop. Foam. Hot towels. A straight razor. What the hell. I told the gentleman to take it off. Clint admitted he liked me better clean shaven. I'd forgotten how I looked without a beard.

Back in the room, we made love again before promptly falling asleep. I awoke a couple hours later and looked at the ceiling. Clint was leaving again tomorrow, and my life would be back in limbo. He didn't have any of the answers I'd hoped he would. Clint awoke and asked what was wrong. I said nothing, but he could tell I was upset. He held me in his arms. I apologized. I felt like a fool, but didn't know what to do. "Wait? Get a job?" He told me to do whatever I thought I should do. That was no help at all. If I knew what to do, I'd have a plan. If I knew what to do, I would be doing it.

Morning came too soon. We made love, but the feeling was melancholy, at least for me. Passion was eclipsed by the parting that was to follow. Good-bye-for-now sex. We showered and got dressed. I took a picture of us in the mirror on the back of the door. We were downstairs by noon for checkout time. I walked Clint to the train. Maybe I could come up there sometime. Clint said that wasn't a good idea. He said he'd call me. That was the last thing he said before stepping on the train. More of the same.

I cried for most of the walk back to the Lawson. A return to the way things had been made me feel utterly forlorn. I bought a bottle of wine at the corner store. I needed to get some idea about what I was doing with my life. Why the heck does love have to be so complicated?

Friday July 21

Hungover. Red wine does it every time. Sad. The blues.

Nothing interesting happened today. All pales in comparison. Gave a quarter to the guy at the corner kiosk for a pack of smokes—the extent of getting out today. Not even reading. My mood lends itself quite well to hiding away and staring at the ceiling and smoking.

Saturday July 22

Ryan came by first thing in the morning. He invited me on a picnic in Lincoln Park. He didn't ask about the time with Clint at all. Strange.

Also found it odd Ryan didn't mention my not having a beard. Maybe he didn't notice. Or maybe he'd already seen me clean shaven. Maybe he'd been watching us more than the one time we saw him. Wanted to ask what he was doing in that office on Wabash. Truthfully, I just wanted to know why he'd been trailing me and who put him up to all this. I wanted to end this charade once and for all.

When he came over to the side of the bed, I found myself wanting him instead. So shallow. I took him into my mouth and pushed him back on the sheets. A few moments later, he was pulling my hair and calling to Jesus. I wiped my mouth with the back of my hand. Now I was ready for a picnic.

Wherever we go, people stare. An older white fellow and a younger colored one. We should have realized our picnic would draw attention. People were actually moving their blankets. Afterward, we walked down to the lagoon. Swan boats. Then a walk through the zoo. More stares. By then, I didn't care.

He finally asked how my time with Clint had been. Here we go, I thought. I said it was nice. I said we'd stayed at the Stevens. I figured I wasn't telling him anything he didn't already know. He asked how things were with Clint's mother and looked like he could have kicked himself. I said fine. Ryan looked relieved. I'm sure I never mentioned Constance to him. Ryan waited a few minutes to bring the conversation around and ask what Clint and I had talked about. I said we didn't talk much. Ryan blushed. Didn't know negroes could do that.

At the far end of the park, men were on the make. By then, Ryan had stripped down to his T-shirt. Those men were eyeing him like something tasty. And some of them were so beautiful.

I said to Ryan, "Look at that. You could have any of these guys. Why me? Why a middle-aged, unemployed, and mostly average man?"

Ryan said he didn't think I was average. Said that in most ways I was above average. In the ways that matter.

I said I was fairly intelligent and let the comment hang. Eventually I added, "Perceptive too." I wanted Ryan to know I wasn't stupid. In some ways, the most maddening thing about all this was I was being treated like a moron who only listened to his sexual urges. That is sometimes accurate. I'm often partial to a hung and handsome man. I was using him. I knew what he wanted, and I knew what I wanted. Sure, a handsome guy can turn my head. But rarely am I blind to everything else. Sometimes, I see the world quite clearly.

Ryan looked at me like he was going to say something more but thought better of it. We kept walking. We circled around the park and went up Diversey to Clark Street. Lots of loitering single men. Smoking. Posed. Eyes revealing everything. Keys at the waist. Keys to everywhere. Keys to nowhere.

Ryan and I took Clark Street all the way back down to the Lawson. Despite the subtext of intrigue, the day was actually quite lovely. I really do enjoy Ryan's company. Maybe that's the point.

Sunday June 23

Irked to discover I'm getting a paunch. Never had a weight problem before, but also have never been unemployed before. Supposedly the middle-age spread comes when one is lax about exercise. My gut has suddenly and decidedly arrived. Need to cut down on sweets. Went to the gym to work up a sweat and ran into Max. I slapped my belly when I saw him.

He laughed and slapped his in reply, then grabbed my hand and rubbed his belly with it and told me to make a wish. "These young guys don't understand," he added.

I said, "They will."

Told him I was aiming to get rid of it. He said he liked me with a bit of meat on my bones. He also said he liked me clean-shaven… or with a beard… or even scruffy. Fat, thin, asleep, and awake. He said he just plain likes me.

Very sweet.

Max and I worked out together for a bit. Told him I needed to find work and mentioned going back to M_____. He asked if I wanted his opinion. I nodded. Max said he doubted they would want me back and reminded me about the brouhaha of my leaving. Had I told Max that whole story? Maybe my memory was growing flabby along with my midsection.

The film came back to the camera store today. Apparently, I'd had this in the camera for some time. So many odds and ends on the roll. Things I didn't recall. A storm. Holiday decorations. The Chicago River dyed green. This year was the second time they'd done it. I didn't get a picture in 1961. The dyeing of the river was the reason I bought the film in the first place. I wanted a photo of it this year. Chicago was the talk of the country on St. Patrick's Day thanks to the plumber's union.

Us.

A shot of Clint turning around on the sidewalk. Another of him sleeping with his muscled, hairy chest in view. Does a man so breathtaking ever doubt his own beauty? Does he live in constant fear of losing his looks? Of knowing the bloom of youth will be gone one day, or does he go through life blithely unaware? Then, one day it's gone and he realizes it. The attention from others wanes. Replaced by another who will one day be replaced. Beauty abandons us just when we need it most. I suppose the secret is not to need it.

The last photo was one of us reflected in the hotel mirror. There we were, smiling above a ball of light. Even though I'm forty-two, there are times when I am quite handsome, even beautiful. Or just photogenic. This was one of those times. The lighting? The angle? Or maybe something else. The comany? My theory is that Clint brought out the attractiveness in me. That day at the Stevens, in the flash of the camera, he gave me a bit of his beauty, a bit of himself.

Monday July 24

Max was right. Filled out a job application at M_____. Got a curt nod of thanks, but no thanks. "We're not looking for anything right now, but we'll keep your application on file." After all those years. Someone else was behind my counter. Saw those jerks from Housewares and Appliances on my way out. They looked the same. Everything looks the same. Ruts rarely change. I was once just as constant, just as unchanging. Depressing, really. Those Housewares jokers opened their bazoos and looked like they were about to say something, but I breezed by as though I didn't see them. Not the most mature way of handling the situation, but boy was it effective.

Clint called.

Constance is responding well to treatment. She should be home in a week. I said I thought she was there. She's been staying at a "rest facility" in Lake Forest. I said nothing because I didn't want to antagonize Clint, but if she wasn't there, why did he have to go back? I was wise to keep quiet. Our talks were too precious to spoil by being contrary or disagreeable. Instead I said I was still walking on a cloud from his visit. He said he was, too. When I asked when he could get away again, he said he had to get going. Voices in the background. Chatter. If Constance was hospitalized, who was there?

The folk singer next door was singing until one in the morning. He seems shy and nice, so I don't want to complain or cause a fuss. Maybe I can just mention to him that the walls are thin and I heard him late last night. He seems like an intelligent kid. Sensitive, if you believe his lyrics. He'll get my meaning. His songs aren't half bad.

Tuesday July 25

Max said they're looking for help at the restaurant. He offered to put in a good word for me. I don't see myself as a waiter. Max reminded me that I needed to see myself as something soon. He was right. Money was running out. I had enough cash for a couple months, but my savings were dwindling. Most men my age were established in a business. Here I was, starting over again. Max reminded me that he had to do the same. There's worse things in life. He was right. The thought of doing something new made me both anxious and excited. The opposite of the M_____ rut. Scary, but with so many possibilities. Limitless really.

For whatever reason, Guys seem to be swarming around me like never before. Men seem even more attracted to me as an older gentleman than when I was younger, middle-age spread and all. An odd and unexpected turn of events. I'd just gotten used to the invisibility of middle age, and lo and behold, life throws me another curve.

Frankie approached me in the hallway right from the shower with a towel wrapped about his torso like a woman. The only guy I've ever seen to wear a towel that way. Frankie said he heard I was looking for work. They're looking for a weekend barback at Jamie's. He said the money was okay. Told him I'd think about it. He said not to think too long, a couple other guys were interested.

I've said it before and I'll say it again. I miss Jack Paar!

Wednesday July 26

Max is putting in a word for me at the Silver Chalice Supper Club. He said I'd probably start with bussing tables. I don't mind. I need money coming in, and the job would keep me occupied. Max said if his boss hired me, I'll need black dress pants and a white shirt. Luckily I still have most of my things from when I worked at M_____. That's all down in storage.

Went for a walk along the lake and marveled once again at the beauty of my hometown. Best skyline anywhere. So many distinctive buildings: the Standard Oil Building, and the Wrigley Building, and the Board of Trade, and 333 North Michigan, and so many others. Hard to imagine what this place was once like, this place the Potawatomi Indians called Chicagoua, named for all the wild garlic that grew along the banks of the river. So much has changed since then. Even the direction of the river's flow has been switched.

Thursday July 27

Someone ransacked my storage space. My things had been thrown about haphazardly. Searched. Nothing seems to have been taken. Nothing I've noticed anyway. Tie clips and cuff links, quite expensive. Untouched. Not sure what they were looking for, but they weren't after valuables.

The vandals didn't touch my clothes, which was fortunate since I was meeting Mr. Scarlotta at the Silver Chalice at four. Max told me about the job interview this morning. We'll see how it goes. Max said Mr. Scarlotta was sympathetic to cases like ours. Mr. Scarlotta has a son who was a homosexual. I was amazed to hear this. Not that his son was that way, but that the father still loved him. Must be quite a guy. Max said the son was away at school.

Mr. Scarlotta is very nice. He hired me bussing tables at the Silver Chalice three nights a week. The pay isn't great, but I wasn't expecting much. If I do well, he promised to promote me to waiter. Then the money will be much better. He shook my hand. Just like that, I'm back in the land of the employed. He said to come in tomorrow around four and someone would show me around. Max came by after his shift to congratulate me. He said it wasn't the best job, but I'd be working with terrific people. "Like me" he added, turning in profile and lifting his nose. Max was a terrific man and a genuine friend. He was someone I could count on.

When I mentioned my storage space had been vandalized, Max said he wasn't surprised. He said the Lawson had been having a lot of problems with theft lately.

I told him nothing was stolen, just ransacked.

Max shook his head. "This place is changing. It's not what it used to be."

I told him I thought it was the world that was changing. "The Lawson is just ahead of the curve or maybe behind it." I wasn't sure of much anymore.

Friday July 28

Still feeling strange after the storage area vandalism. One thing I did find in the storage area was my birthday book. Flipped open the page for today. Noted: Today is Ella Nash's birthday. Ella! The woman I used to work with at M_____. Why had I bothered to make a note of her birthday? We scarcely exchanged five words in all the time I knew her. She was never a friend. Never even very nice. Frequently dismissive. Sometimes insulting. A crass gossipmonger. Odd to consider how I relied on my job for social needs. If I searched, I'm sure I would find all the M_____ people in here. Even Reginald and Nick from Housewares and Appliances. Even some movie stars were included: Marilyn, Ida Lupino, Liz Taylor, Arlene Dahl, Lucy.

Dreamt of my mother last night. She died so long ago. We were strolling through a park, and I was holding her hand. I didn't look at her face, but I knew she was my mother from the way she held my hand. I wanted to look up. I wanted to see her face. The sun was so bright. I could only see the shadow of her. Don't know if my dream was a surfacing memory or my imagination.

Saturday July 29

Last night at the Silver Chalice went well. Bussing tables requires speed and attentiveness. Scarlotta seemed pleased with my performance. By the end of the night, I was a pro. After closing, we all gathered at the bar and had a beer. Boy but that was swell. Max said the folks who close every night have a cocktail as a sort of ritual. Tradition. They all clinked longneck bottles and welcomed me. Camaraderie. These fellows already merit having their birthdays written down in my book. As Max intimated, many of the staff were queers.

Clint called when I was getting ready before work. Told him I just started at the Silver Chalice. He said he missed me. Said I missed him too, but I had to go. He is coming back into town next week. He lowered his voice and said he thought he knew why all this was happening. I knew just what he meant by this. He had remembered something key. I asked what he was talking about, but he said Not now. I told him I worked Wednesdays, Fridays, and Saturdays. He promised to call tomorrow with the specifics of when he'd be in town.

Two minutes later, Max was at my door. As we were leaving for work, we saw Ryan in the hall. He asked where I was headed all dressed up, and I told him I had a job. On the elevator down, Max mentioned the look that crossed Ryan's face when I said I was working. I was too rushed to notice. Max said Ryan almost looked panicked. Why should he care? I had no idea what that could be about. Maybe Max was being overly dramatic.

I told Max about Clint's call.

Sunday July 30

Hungover. The shift ended with a staff beer. Then a bunch of us went to Shoreline 7 and then Jamie's. Frankie was giving us shots every other minute. Holy Toledo those restaurant people know how to drink. A fun and lively bunch. Most of those guys just fracture me. Before I knew it, the bartender gave last call.

Ryan came by this morning to tell me he was moving out. His job starts tomorrow, and he was moving to a place on Farragut. So, was that all true? He didn't give me his new address. I wished him well. His behavior was different. He stayed close to the door the entire time. Didn't make a pass at me. Looked afraid that I'd make a pass at him, Hardly looked me in the eye. Odd. Maybe he realized this could never work out. We were both partnered, even though distance made both relationships difficult. Ryan and I came together out of need and want, but those sorts of things come to an end. Most relationships do. Maybe there was a more sinister explanation for Ryan's behavior. Maybe he'd changed because his mission was complete or had been aborted. Or maybe he kept his distance because I smelled like someone who had closed the bars a few hours ago.

Clint called an hour or so later. Said he would meet me at the Lodge Tavern on Division in a couple of hours. I took a steam and a shower. Felt relatively human by the time I walked in the faux English-style place near Division and Rush. Clint waved me over to his booth. He rose as I approached and slapped me on the shoulder.

Very buddy-like. I hate that we can't embrace. Hoped we'd make up for it later. "What a Wonderful World" by Sam Cooke was on the jukebox. Clint looked exhausted. He was already drinking. I ordered ginger ale.

Once we got our drinks, Clint leaned close. He was through pussyfooting around. He said one of his father's business associates from the army had been by the house. "I'll call him Uncle Gene." Clint said he had a couple cocktails in him, and by the time he saw Uncle Gene, he'd had enough of all this cloak and dagger stuff. "I took Uncle Gene into the library and put him up against a wall and asked if he knew why I was being tailed." He asked what Clint meant. "Uncle Gene, you've known me since I was a kid." I guess Gene went over and closed the door. Said he didn't approve of the things Clint was doing. "Your father would roll over in his grave."

Clint reminded him that the General was cremated. He added that he didn't care what his father would think. He told Uncle Gene he knew damn well that wasn't what this was about anyway.

Uncle Gene asked what Clint knew about Cuba. Clint said not too much. Castro and casinos. Gene said certain parties were worried that Clint had overheard or seen certain things when he contaminated his father's business meeting in Paris. Contaminated? Uncle Gene said that by coming to the room that day, he'd caused a gross security breach. Clint said he instantly knew Uncle Gene was talking about the day in Paris when he'd returned to the room after forgetting his wallet. However, Clint said he hadn't seen anything. Uncle Gene said the parties involved couldn't take that chance. Certain parties didn't know how long Clint had been listening at the door. Clint reiterated that he hadn't heard anything, he'd simply forgotten his wallet. Nothing more.

Gene said that was unfortunate and that didn't matter much now. Wheels were in motion. Everything was already underway. "These people don't take chances. They can't afford to. To them, practically nothing is too much. They've made their minds up about you and your boyfriend."

Clint asked for the truth. Said he was owed that much.

"Soon it'll all go public anyway." Gene told Clint if he breathed a word, he'd be in trouble. Clint said he already was. The operation was about missile silos the Russians were installing in Cuba. Certain people were worried Clint knew about it and might have told his "male friend." People fear the two of you might be connected. Homosexuals are high risk for security leaks. We can't let the Russians know we've been spying."

Homosexual was all but synonymous with communist.

Clint finished his beer and looked me square in the eye. "They thought you were coaxing the secret out of me or that we had teamed to sell information. When we ran, it all but confirmed their theories."

"Why wouldn't we run? We were being threatened."

Clint shrugged. He said that was something else entirely. "Mother was having us followed. She was heavily sedated when she came back home this week and admitted it to me. She never told the General. She said she didn't want to lose me."

At least I was somewhat on target about that. I asked about Ryan and Preston. Clint nodded. He'd asked Uncle Gene about them as well. The two men were undercover operatives carefully selected and placed to find out what each of us knew, to keep tabs on us, and to determine if we had any contact with communist sympathizers.

I asked if they were really queer, and Clint just shrugged. If not, Ryan was very convincing. I hope he got a medal and a fat bonus for his thoroughness and commitment.

Ryan asked what I thought.

I said I wondered if they killed his father too.

Clint said he doubted it.

I didn't know what else to say. This was like a science-fiction thriller. I couldn't think. Strangely my focus was on the Connie Francis song playing on the jukebox. "Everybody's Somebody's Fool".

Clint said we needed to run again. "They know that I know. And now Uncle Gene has disappeared."

Tears were in my eyes. I loved him, but I was trying to get my life back together. I didn't know if I could throw it all away and start running again.

Clint said these interested parties were relentless. They knew he had been told about things. Clint said that was why Ryan had suddenly moved out. "And Preston vanished too." No more need to dig. They know that I know. And suspect we both know. Now they need to keep us quiet."

"But you said we wouldn't say anything."

"It doesn't matter. I've been around these types all my life. They won't believe us. They don't take chances. They need to be certain."

I lit a cigarette and took Clint's hand. To blazes with who saw me and what they thought. I loved him, but I was tired. He looked me in the eyes and knew my answer. He knew I'd had enough. He said he understood, but he couldn't take that chance. He said he'd spotted a suspicious-looking fellow at the bar, and they probably had someone else watching us now. He said after I finished my cigarette, I should get up and go out the door. "Leave without looking back. Without a second glance. As though we'll see each other again."

I had tears in my eyes.

Clint continued, "Spend the next few hours in crowded places." Clint said he was the one they really wanted anyway. "If they question you, it will probably be about my whereabouts. Best if you don't know."

I didn't know if I could walk away.

Clint grabbed my cigarette and snubbed it out in the ashtray. "Now go. You mustn't look like anything has happened."

How was I supposed to do that?

Clint took his hand away. "I love you. I always will. Just go, and don't turn around."

"I love you too," I said, rising from the table.

Monday July 31

Nothing makes sense. After getting outside and rounding the corner, I knew I was being a fool. What had I done? Walking out on the best thing I ever had. How could I be so stupid? My life was nothing before Clint. I didn't want to go back to living that way because I was too afraid to be with him. I was doing the one thing I swore I would never do. By leaving him, I was proving that I didn't deserve him.

Instead of heading anywhere, I walked quickly around the block. By the time I was almost back to the Lodge I was running. Looked in the door of the bar. Gone. Ran to check the restroom. Not there. Shit! Would he go back home? Was he already on the run? I suspected the latter. I didn't see a suitcase. Maybe it was under the table or already stowed someplace. If only I'd asked more questions. Had more time to think. If only I hadn't been so afraid, so eager to return to normalcy. A routine. I ran back to the Lawson and packed a bag. Two minutes later, I was headed for Union Station.

Wednesday August 2

When Clint didn't show at the train station after two hours, I headed to the Greyhound terminal on Randolph. I recognized one of the guys at the counter. From Jamie's? Shoreline 7? He recognized me. We didn't acknowledge the mutual recognition with anything more than a smile. His name tag said Ron. I approached and flashed the picture of Clint turning around on the sidewalk. I asked Ron if he'd seen him. Ron nodded. He'd been in earlier. He showed the picture to his colleague who said something to Ron. Clint had been asking about a bus to Milwaukee. Ron said it didn't leave for two hours. I thanked him and took a seat on the bench.

Clint didn't show for that bus. There was another at six in the morning. With hours to kill, I headed to the State Theater. The movies were a bottom-of-the-barrel triple bill: Tarzan Goes to India, the US/Japan horror film The Manster, and a Roger Corman thing called The Intruder. I played around in the balcony a bit with a thin Italian fellow. Nervous energy. I'd go out of my mind otherwise. I tried to sleep a bit. At five, somebody threw a popcorn box at my head and told me to stop snoring. I should've thanked the guy. Otherwise I might have overslept.

Clint was in line when I returned to the station. I'd recognize those broad shoulders and muscle butt anywhere. He wore a windbreaker and khakis. I tapped him on the shoulder. He turned and smiled. I could tell he wanted to do more. Kiss me. Embrace me. Instead, he shook my hand. He saw my suitcase. I sidled beside him and said I hoped he could use a travel companion. The look in his eyes said it all.

We bought tickets and waited beside the vending machines. I apologized about before. I said I should never have gotten up from that booth. I was being afraid instead of being true to my heart. Clint understood. He said he had money this time and nodded to the briefcase beside his duffel bag. I asked him where he got it. Clint said he didn't take a cent that he wasn't owed.

I wasn't sure what he meant by that.

The sun was already blazing when the bus pulled from the terminal. We were two of six passengers. We sat near the back. Felt so good to be putting distance between us and that craziness. In Milwaukee, we rented a place near the station. Clint said he had to sleep. He must've been exhausted. He was asleep by noon and slept until evening. He called me over to the bed. Quiet. Aroused. Ready. He began slowly, but took me savagely. I had to tell him to take it easy a couple times. Clint apologized. He needed it. Needed me. Needed to feel something. Badly. Desperately. He claimed he'd never wanted anyone more.

Afterward, I slept until morning.

Thursday August 3

Clint said we couldn't afford to be stupid about things. "If they wanted to, they could charge us with treason." Treason. When I said that wasn't true, Clint said it didn't matter. He said there were prisoners in the jail cells of every state who'd done nothing but be in the wrong place at the wrong time. I couldn't imagine President Kennedy going along with doings like this. Clint said Kennedy didn't have to know. Clint said autonomous parts of the government operated outside of the law. He added, "They could lock us up and throw away the key. Who would save us? My mother is incapacitated, and you don't have any family."

This seemed the wrong time to admit that I'd lied before. I wasn't raised in a foundling home. I had a father and brother. I'd no idea why I lied to him in the first place. Things were different then. I was different then. Keeping secrets does that to a person after a while. Makes lying a habit. No one is to be trusted. Lying isn't about being dishonest, it's about protection. Constantly hiding who you are makes truth the enemy. But I had never lied to Clint about how I felt. I didn't lie about love.

Ever.

Clint stayed in the hotel room all day. He can't risk being seen. He's formulating a plan. I was going stir-crazy and must've smoked a full pack of cigarettes. Eventually, I went out and got us something to eat, a few books, a deck of cards, and another pack of smokes. Things are different this time. Being underground the first time had been risky, but it felt more like an adventure. This time it feels more like survival.

Friday August 4

I told Clint we had to do something. We can't just sit here. He said he had to think. I told him he'd said that yesterday. He glared at me. For a moment, he frightened me. I was being a nag. I wondered if I did the right thing joining him. Maybe I should have gone back to the Lawson and tried to build a new life for myself. With someone else? With Max? The moment passed…

I looked over at Clint on the bed. He patted the spot beside him. What was I thinking? How could I have ever doubt my decision? This is where I belong. Beside the man I love. I curled into him and said he was tense. He kissed the top of my head. I licked down his body and took him in my mouth. He toyed with my hair. He needed this so badly. So did I. My man. Myself. We were a team. Being together was what mattered. Clint clenched his thighs. Released. He said he loved me and fell back on the pillows. I watched him sleep. The fluttering of lashes on his closed lids. The rise and fall of his chest. The periodic twitches here and there. Next thing I knew it was morning.

Over the past two days, I have read two Agatha Christie mysteries, Murder in Mesopotamia and Sparkling Cyanide.

Saturday August 5

I told Clint we couldn't stay here forever.

He said we could afford to stay here a long time. He asked me to hand him the briefcase. He flipped the latches and opened the lid. Money. Bundles of bills in rows. Thousands. More cash than I'd ever seen. I didn't want to know where it came from. I had to stop myself from asking. I knew too much already.

Clint fell back asleep. I got up, brushed my teeth, took my journal and smokes, and left a note that I was going to get coffee and read. I kissed Clint on the cheek as I left the room. He looked at peace. Hadn't seen him looking that way in a while.

When I returned, Clint was sitting on the bed. He said we were leaving Milwaukee next Tuesday. He said the best way to slip into Canada was through the boundary waters of Minnesota. No border patrol there. "Easy as taking a canoe ride." He seemed positive. More focused. His mood was contagious. Having a direction feels good.

Sunday August 6

Marilyn is dead.

The headline was the first thing I saw when I went down to the lobby. Pills nearby. Thirty-six years old. Found nude. Facedown in her bed. I feel so unbearably sad. When I came back to the room and told Clint the news, I was already crying. I read The Milwaukee Journal article word for word and then went out and bought the New York Times, the Los Angeles Times, the Chicago Tribune, and got more cigarettes. The coverage was all over the television. Everyone is heartbroken and in shock. Even her harshest critics have become turncoats.

Odd that her passing should feel so devastating, but sometimes people in films seem more real to me than the people in everyday life, and Marilyn was my favorite. So much sweetness and beauty and vulnerability. Today felt like the end of innocence. And the start of a much darker era.

Monday August 7

Clint said we should plan on leaving tomorrow. I nodded. I was still thinking about Marilyn. I kissed him and said I'd be right back. He told me he loved me.

I went down to the magazine stand to see if there was anything new. The tabloids were already having a field day. Even mainstream papers were splashed with her image, promising new and sordid details. When I got back to the room, the door was open. I looked around. Clint was gone. Voices. Strange men.

"Joseph Hoagland?" they said.

I nodded.

Stupid!

I should've said no. I should've run. They took me by either arm. Clint had already been taken. They wouldn't say where. They ushered me downstairs and out a back entrance of the hotel. They covered my head with a burlap bag. We drove quite a ways. I heard one of the men rifling through my bag.

"Looks clean," he finally said to the driver. The other didn't respond.

From the feel of the terrain, we'd pulled off the highway and onto a side road. More turns. They removed the bag. The road had dead-ended. The men escorted me to a low cement building. Two guards at the entrance. Two more guards just inside. No one looked at me.

They pushed me into a cell and threw my bag in afterward. They ignored my questions about what was going on. About Clint. About everything. I demanded to speak with a lawyer. They'd already left the building.

Two guards were stationed in the office at the end of the hall. A toilet was in a corner of my cell. A sink stood beside it. The walls are cement block. No window. Hours later, they brought a bologna sandwich.

Later:

Don't know how many days have passed, but I don't crave cigarettes anymore. My caffeine headaches are gone.

A week?

Longer?

The only way to gauge time is by the coming and going of the guards. No one has told me anything. I've grown hoarse from asking. No one has even spoken to me. I worry about Clint constantly. No one here acknowledges me. The fluorescent lights never dim. They want me in custody, but don't seem to want anything from me. If only I had some word about Clint, I would feel a thousand times better.

If only…

Later:

I've read the Agatha Christie books in my bag a half-dozen times each. Yesterday, I gave them to one of the guards. When he came in today, he gave me The Adventures of Augie March by Saul Bellow, a worn copy of Babbitt by Sinclair Lewis, and a Dorothy Sayers mystery. He said he didn't see the harm in it and that if I behaved myself he would bring me more later. Those were the first words anyone has spoken to me here. The first acknowledgement. The first hint of compassion I've been shown since my incarceration. I asked about Clint. He ignored me.

Later:

They have a television in the office. One of the guards is a bit hard of hearing. Sometimes I catch bits of things. He watches the Three Stooges most of the time. A couple times, I heard the Bonanza theme. Still no word about Clint or how long they plan on holding me. I've seen no one in charge here. There seems to be no one except the guards and me.

Later:

There is a mouse in here as well. I heard him earlier.

Later:

These blasted lights are driving me crazy. Maybe that's the intent. I used to think I was a loner. Now I'm not so sure. I relive a lot of scenes and memories in my mind. I worry about Clint. Wonder if he is someplace similar. Maybe he's in a different part of this building. There's no way of knowing anything more about where I'm being held.

Saw the mouse today. He is gray and was on the other side of the hallway. He ran when he heard a guard approach. I worry the guard saw him and is going to set a trap.

Later:

Thank goodness for the Reader. That's what I call the kind guard since I don't know his name. Everyone is nameless here. I'm sure he's been forbidden to converse with me. Probably risking his job with the few words he's spoken. He drops the books inside the bars when he brings dinner. Today he gave me The Caine Mutiny and Marjorie Morningstar by Herman Wouk and King's Row by Henry Bellamann. Although he is one of my captors, I sense that he's kind. I need to believe that. The food is horrid. Bologna sandwiches. Tuna sandwiches. Sometimes peanut butter and jelly sandwiches. Sometimes I just get toast and a banana. I give a bit of the crust to the mouse. He waits near the bars after my dinner tray comes. Apparently the guard never saw him. He needs a name. Homer?

What I wouldn't give for a toothbrush.

Later:

I've felt so horrible lately. I wonder if they're putting something in my sandwiches. A slow poison. Why not just kill me? Doubtful about the poisoning theory. After all, Homer seems fine. Maybe Homer has grown immune to poisons. Maybe the poison is not in the bread. I suspect I've read too many mysteries.

Later:

The pains are horrible. It's difficult to breathe or even hold the pen. In case this is the end, I love you, Clint. Always have. Always will.

Later:

I awoke in some sort of clinic. No windows. A bed pan with a red cross on it. No toilet. Some sort of operation has been completed. There's a scar on my abdomen. I suspect it was my appendix. There is no one to tell me.

Even here, I am alone.

I wonder if I'll simply be transported back to my cell. Ironic they went to the trouble of saving me. I suspect they need to be convinced of their own righteousness. Letting me die would make them inhumane. But to hold me without counsel or trial makes them good Americans. We all need to be the heroes of our own stories, I suppose.

Tuesday October 23

As quickly as it began, it ended. My captors drove me to Appleton and bought me a one-way ticket to Chicago. I was told no one would believe me if I said anything. I was told that if I mentioned it to anyone, I would return. Indefinitely. Or worse.

Or worse?

They didn't need to hold me any longer. People were hysterical. Crackpots were shouting on every other street corner. No one would listen to me. News of the Cuban Missile Crisis was everywhere. The tension and horror was palpable.

The newspaper headline at the bus station read Nuclear War Imminent.

President Kennedy announced last night the existence of nuclear missiles in Cuba. There was going to be a showdown. The cat is out of the proverbial bag. Even if I knew anything, no one would listen. Everyone was too terrified to hear. When I mentioned Clint to the man taking me to the bus, he just smirked. What did that mean? Was that a comment on our relationship or on Clint's fate? I could've killed that bastard with my bare hands, but I wanted freedom too badly.

My reflection in the bus bathroom mirror was startling. I'd lost a good twenty pounds and I've aged a decade. I wonder how much a few good meals and some sunlight will change. Maybe I've been damaged beyond repair. I'll get through this. Queers are tougher and more resilient than they suspect. We're forever under attack. Every week, we need to make the decision to be a survivor. Their punishment was unique only in its severity. They consider us vermin, but vermin are difficult to destroy.

Homer is probably still roaming those halls.

Wednesday October 24

Back at the Lawson, but everything is different. Maybe it's only me. I waited in the lobby for Max. He came through the revolving door an hour later. He took both my hands and asked what happened. "You don't look so good."

I said he didn't want to know.

He said the world was going to explode so it didn't much matter. I think he was making a joke, but I couldn't think clearly. I needed to get myself together. I needed to find Clint.

I asked him to buy me a pack of smokes. My wallet had been emptied when I was imprisoned. He gave me change for the vending machine. The first cigarette made me dizzy.

Max said he had something for me. "When I first got it, I worried because it meant you two weren't together." Max said it was a letter from Clint.

We went to his room. Max had taped the letter behind a picture on the wall. He handed me the envelope. The letter was dated two months ago, soon after we'd been apprehended. I assumed the return address on Maple in Wilmette was Clint's home, or at least the place where his mother lived.

Clint opened by saying he hoped this letter would find me. He was being held against his will in some sort of medical facility. They thought he knew everything. He'd failed to convince them otherwise. He was scared. Clint said he wasn't sure what was going to happen. He'd overheard them talking about a procedure. A guarantee that he won't talk. Clint convinced one of his captors to mail this letter. He said the hope of this getting to me gave him some peace. Clint said he loved me, that he always would. He was sorry things had turned out the way they did. "Maybe in a different time…" He said he remembered my every expression. Every inch of my body. He said in some ways, we never stood a chance, but we made the impossible possible. At least for a while. "Our love should've been so much easier." He repeated that he loved me deeply and completely and always would. He asked forgiveness for getting me involved in all this.

Clint should've known that I still thought loving him was worth it. Always would. Some might call me insane, but I wouldn't trade a single moment of our time together.

I held up the letter to Max, "They've done something to him."

Max asked what.

I didn't know, but I was going to find out. I needed sleep. Max said I could sleep in his bed. He'd take the floor. "Or we can share the bed if you like." I thanked him for the offer, but I was too exhausted for anything more than sleep. Max understood. Max always understood. He gave me the bed and he took the floor. He gave me the lasagna he brought home from his lunch shift at the restaurant. Best food I've ever tasted.

Thursday October 25

News drones on about the missile crisis. Panic. Fear. Dread. Probable war. Possible annihilation. The rockets are so near US soil. The flip of a switch. The press of a button. So close to nuclear war. Many are calling it Armageddon. The end of days. Church attendance is through the roof. Bars are packed. Lines for confession, communion, baptism, and sacraments in general. Work absenteeism is astronomical as are weddings and suicides. Two men were reported walking down Michigan Avenue holding hands. They were arrested a half mile later. End of the world… and this is still the crime worth punishing. Everyone is very quiet on the streets and in the hallways, tiptoeing about as though monastic silence will protect them. Personally, I don't care. Please God, don't let the missile strike until I see Clint again. That's all I ask. Today I'm taking the train to Wilmette.

Friday October 26

Wilmette. As I walked down Maple Avenue, I couldn't help but notice the changing leaves. Trees the color of fire. Much of that is lost in the city. I found the address and prepared an elaborate ruse to get inside. Instead, when I approached their home, I saw a walkway to the backyard. And Clint was there. He was seated with his back to me, facing a trio of trees all yellow and orange. I couldn't believe it. After all this time and worry, there he was.

I ran through the crunch of leaves. As I neared, I could sense something was wrong. I could feel it. Him, and yet not him. Dear God! I knelt beside his chair. An afghan was across his lap. Clint was withering. His skin was chalky. A bit of drool hung from his lips. His hands were quivering. The worst, by far, were his vacant eyes. I saw the scar peeking out from beneath the brim of his cap. I was no fool. I knew what the procedure had been and the irrevocable damage that had been done. My poor Clint. I took his hand. Limp. Slaughter would've been more humane. What have they done to you? They've destroyed the man I loved. Drilled into his skull and removed the secrets that they feared he'd had. They'd been wrong. His secrets were of a different nature.

The men who'd done this were nothing but paranoid. They're always so frightened of our kind. Terrified of the vague threat we pose to the American way of life. What was that anyway? The great irony in all this was that he'd never known their secret, and this Cuban crisis had happened anyway.

At that moment, I wished I had access to the switch or the button that controlled the annihilation of this society and the men who've done this. To blazes with all of you. My world had already been destroyed in a flash of a scalpel. I wanted the earth to suffer as well and experience the annihilation that came with a flash of detonation followed by a mushroom cloud. Let those bastards responsible for this experience doom.

Constance came onto the back patio. Maybe she'd been there all along. Seeing Clint had made me blind with horror. Then blind with rage. She was flanked by two men in medical attire with guns. The men took a few steps toward me. Constance said something to them I couldn't hear. She approached alone. I was still sitting at Clint's knees and holding one of his hands. Only the hint of muscle remained. It shook with a slight palsy. Constance was there. I could see her feet and the hem of her orange coat. I didn't know what to say. Eventually she remarked that Clint had always loved the changing of the leaves.

He was beyond enjoyment. I asked if his love of autumn colors was why she had him pushed here. I looked at the flatness of his eyes and the drool on his chin. "He doesn't even know where he is, or who he is." I finally screamed. "Is that what you wanted?"

She shook her head. Pharmaceutically calm. She said it wasn't her doing. "I didn't want to lose him, but I never wanted this to happen. I tried to stop them. You must believe me."

I said nothing. Why should I believe her? And why should she possibly care whether I believe her or not? I said she must be very happy to have her little boy back. "Now he'll never leave you." Cruel. I wanted my words to hurt her. I hope they festered inside her like cancer. I wanted to walk away, but I couldn't.

"Couldn't you convince them he knew nothing?"

She shook her head no. "They thought his wanting to leave Paris meant he knew something. They didn't know he wanted to get back to you. When they found out, it only made things worse. Returning to a homosexual lover only strengthened their argument."

I didn't believe her. She could have cleared things up. She could have said something.

Constance said by then it was already too late. When we ran from the Lawson, she had us trailed because she wanted to bring us back. "Running was proof to them that you knew something. I had to find you first." Constance was afraid of what would happen if they got their hands on us, on Clint. Her fears were well-founded.

Constance was rubbing her hands together. She looked much older than I remembered. She said if she could change the past, she would. She put a hand on Clint's shoulder and said she just wanted what was best for him. That's what she'd always wanted. She had tears in her eyes. She said she was only trying to protect him. "I just wanted him to be safe, to be happy."

She or the General could have done something.

She reiterated that she'd done all she could, but we kept running and tensions surrounding Cuba continued to escalate. The powers behind this couldn't afford to take any chances. Constance said her boy loved this country. And he would have understood. "I think he does now, don't you?"

I hated her so. Constance didn't have the slightest knowledge of who her son really was or what made him happy. I said I pitied her for that. "You knew the son you wanted to know, but you never knew the great man that I did."

Her lips thinned. "You only knew one sordid side of him."

I looked at Clint and then away. "He was happy. We were happy. But his happiness wasn't the kind you wanted. It didn't fit, did it?" Constance was crying. I was being a monster. I had to lash out at someone. Constance didn't do this. She loved her son, but she didn't accept him. Her crime was more common than not.

After a silence, I said I didn't blame her, but I wasn't the one she had to answer to. "You wanted to control your son and now you can." The ache inside me was so deep, I was beyond caring. I wanted my words to scar her, to scramble her brain. I was crying. Had I been crying all along? "There had to be some other solution."

Constance shook her head. "I begged for him. They told me if I didn't keep quiet, I'd have the same. These people will do whatever it takes." Constance glanced at the men near the patio doors. Panic flashed in her eyes. Was she afraid they heard her? "Please, don't think this is my doing. I've said too much already."

Something in the way she spoke made me suddenly feel for her. I apologized. She wasn't the enemy. Constance was broken as well. Despite how much I wanted to blame and hate her, I believed her. She couldn't have wanted this for her son. What mother could? I reached for Constance's hand and gripped it.

The gesture would have made Clint happy.

Constance let go of my hand. She looked once more at the armed men near the patio door. "There's no place for you here. No future."

She was forceful, but I suspected she was protecting me. She was asking me to save myself. That meant walking away from the past. Weeks before, my life had been filled with promise. Hope. A future. Now there is nothing.

Nothing.

The man I loved is gone. Annihilated. Removed with a single slice. His husk is here, yet the person I loved has been destroyed. Clint has become a ghost. I have no legal right to be here or to hold him.

She said I was welcome to visit now and again. "But there's nothing here," she repeated. Constance sounded less than fragile. "I'm doing what he would have wanted. He wouldn't want this life for you." She turned once more to the men on the porch before turning back to me. Go, she mouthed.

Constance was right. A great man would have seen it as his duty to stay. A great man would have stayed and fought her and found satisfaction with the memory of the man that was there. For a great man, the memory would be enough.

That isn't me.

I'm not a great man or a cinema hero. I'm an ordinary guy. I'm someone who'd known great love. With Clint by my side, I was great. But that is over. My greatness, like his, has been undone by a scalpel.

I bent over and kissed Clint good-bye.

Forever.

They say all relationships must end eventually.

Don't judge me too harshly for walking away. I've never been one for empty sentiment. This is no time to romanticize the situation or pray for a miracle. I have to be realistic. This wasn't the cinema. There is no happy ending to this tale. Irrevocable is a word void of hope. But a tragic end doesn't diminish what we had. If anything, it enhances its brilliance.

Often the brightest lights cannot be sustained.

Staying would be futile. Pointless sacrifice. An act of lunacy rather than bravery. I am no fool. I can't afford to be. None of us can. All I ever wanted is to be happy. There was no hope for happiness or fulfillment here, for any of us. Part of being happy is knowing when to walk away. Thanks to Clint, I am no longer afraid of life, or love. Knowing him has changed me. Being part of the magic that was "us" changed me.

Forever.

Irrevocable.

My sweet man. I'll always love him.

Always.

Forever.

Thank God for this journal, for allowing me to capture and remember every bit of our time together. A blessing.

Monday October 29

Back at the Lawson. The international crisis has ended. Disaster has been averted. The Soviets have withdrawn the missiles from Cuban soil.

Kennedy is a hero.

The end of time was easier to face than the thought of life going on.

Wednesday, November 7

Almost feels as though I've run out of words. As though life and experience have muted me. There's nothing but silence in my life. An absence. Flipping through these pages, I only see Clint. Even when we were apart, he was with me. A part of me. I have nothing more to add. No more words. No more addendum to our story.

My story is something else entirely.

Where do I go from here? How do I live with such a void, an emptiness where there was once fulfillment? I considered throwing myself from the roof of this place like so many had done before me, but that would only tarnish Clint's memory.

He'd want me to live. I have to believe that.

Love is not selfish.

Loves goes deeper than possessiveness.

Clint would want me to try to find love again. If the situation were reversed, I would wish the same for him.

Not sure about love. Not being alone sounds nice. Maybe companionship. Friendship. Camaraderie. All worthy. All admirable. All things that make live livable, but not magical. Maybe one day love will appear again, just as unexpectedly as it had come before.

Monday November 12

Second chances?

Max is getting a place on Augusta Street a few blocks from here. He asked me to move in with him. I like Max a great deal. I always have. Maybe now the time is right.

We share so many things. He's lost a great deal as well. Mostly, after all we've been through, we both share a wish not to be so alone. There isn't the magic I had with Clint, but Max and I need each other. Needing and being needed have their own rewards.

I never had that with Clint. Not sure he ever needed me.

Max is a friend and a companion. At one time he was a lover and he may be my lover again. Maybe one day I'll grow to love him. Maybe. He is a kind man. With age, I've come to realize that kindness is perhaps the most important quality. And he's sexy too.

Max has no illusions. He knows that Clint will always be the love of my life. Max understands. Max has his demons as well. He doesn't want to replace Clint. He's not asking me to forget the past or for anything more than I'm willing to give. He says that's enough, for now. Max is a patient man as well.

Moving seems like a healthy choice. I can't stay at the Lawson any longer. Too many ghosts roam these halls. Rather, there is one ghost, but that ghost is everywhere.

I need to remember the love Clint and I shared. Lunches in the park. Quiet days in bed. His furry chest.

Listening to his heart beat. His laugh. His eager touch. Those hands. Those lips. The weight of him. The all of him. The feel of him inside me. I need to remember what we had and not what happened. Gratitude is my greatest consolation as well as my greatest challenge. Supposedly it will overcome sorrow in time. That's what I'm told anyway. A change of venue might hasten the process.

Max holds me when I'm feeling blue.

And I return the favor.

Clint and I had something incredible. Our time together changed my life. Forever. Maybe I have the potential to change my life again with someone. If that is anyone, it's Max.

When I told Max I'd move in with him, he kissed me. And I kissed him back. The passion is there.

Maybe I'll regret things in a week or a month. Maybe I'll regret moving in with Max five minutes after leaving the Lawson. Life comes with our breath, but being alive comes from taking chances. I'd lived for so long playing it safe. I was fearful of making a mistake.

Being wrong.

Looking foolish.

I watched life pass me by while waiting to be certain about my career, my relationships, about everything. Clint pulled me to my feet. He made me stand and caused me to realize that waiting to be certain means waiting indefinitely. Life is too short. Too precious. Life is not a waiting game.

Failure is easier to live with than regret.

Maybe I'm not through changing. I suspect I never will be, not if I'm open. Not if I remain willing.

If experience has taught me anything, it's that life holds great promise but offers no guarantees.

When I flipped to the back of the journal an envelope fell to the floor along with three pictures. The first photo was of Clint, a dark-haired beauty turning around on the sidewalk and wearing a look of surprise. There was another picture, this one of Clint asleep. A handsome man with his powerful chest exposed. The last photo was of Clint and Joseph. This was the shot taken in the mirror. Their heads were tilted together and the burst of light from the flashbulb exploded before them. The flash looked like the brilliance of the men combined. They were different than I had imagined them. They looked like men you might see every day. I opened the envelope.

August 15

Dear Joseph,

I pray this letter finds you. As you have no doubt realized, I was apprehended in Milwaukee. There was a knock on the door, and I opened it thinking you'd forgotten your key. Instead it was five agents. Before I could react, two had my arms behind me and were leading me away. They cuffed me. A third drove me back toward Chicago. They shot me up with something, and I lost consciousness. I believe I'm being held in some sort of medical facility on the far north side.

When I regained consciousness, they questioned me. I was interrogated for hours. They thought I was withholding valuable secrets. They think I sold the information. I assured them that the money I had in the hotel room was from my father's home safe. I said if wrongful deeds had been done to get that money, it was my father's doing, not mine. They belted me repeatedly for attempting to tarnish the great General's reputation.

I'm not sure what is going to happen to me. I fear the worst and heard the word procedure whispered last night. I have no idea if I was intended to hear it. Maybe it was a threat, a ploy to get information. Or maybe they think it's the best way to minimize any threat I might pose. I heard mother out there. She was distraught. Hysterical. They refused to let her see me.

I've convinced one of the orderlies here to mail this for me. My hope, that this letter eventually finds its way to you, gives me strength.

I love you. I never understood the meaning of love until I met you. I'd felt lust and infatuation before, but never love. With you, it was never purely physical. I felt a spiritual connection, an emotional bond, and something almost magical. Maybe in a different time our love would have been easier. I'm so sorry things turned out the way they did. I remember everything about you, Joseph. I remember your smile and your frown and your slightly peeved expression. I loved them all. I remember every curve and inch of your body.

I'm so pained by the way things have turned out. You didn't deserve any of this. We didn't deserve this. Not one bit. In some ways, we never stood a chance, but sometimes love blooms in a treacherous place. Sometimes that only enhances love's beauty.

I'm not hopeful about my future. I know these people. They are vile and ruthless. I've heard stories about how they operate.

Maybe we will see one another again sometime. If not in this lifetime, then in the next. I love you deeply and I always will.

Always.

Please forgive me for getting you involved in all this.

With all my heart forever,
Clint

Trademarks Acknowledgment –

The author acknowledges the trademark status and trademark owners of the following places and items mentioned in this work of fiction:

Woolworth's – 6819 Real Estate LLC
Crisco – Procter & Gamble Co.
Falstaff – Falstaff Brewing Corporation
Campbell's – CSC Brands LP
20th Century Fox – 20th Century Fox Film Corp.

Owen Keehnen

In addition to his newest novels, The Matinee Idol and Love Underground, writer and historian Owen Keehnen is the author of the humorous gay novel Young Digby Swank, the gay novel The Sand Bar, and the horror novel Doorway Unto Darkness. Keehnen has had his fiction, essays, columns and interviews appear in dozens of magazines and anthologies worldwide and authored the reference book The LGBT Book of Days. He is currently in charge of LGBTQ content for the Chicago tourism website, Choose Chicago. Keehnen is the co-founder and senior biographer of the LGBT organization, The Legacy Project (LegacyProjectChicago.org) which seeks to bring proper recognition to LGBT people and their contributions throughout history. He co-authored Leatherman: The Legend of Chuck Renslow, Jim Flint: The Boy From Peoria, and Vernita Gray: From Woodstock to the White House with Tracy Baim. He is also the author of several M/M ebook novellas for Wilde City. Over 100 of his 1990s interviews with various LGBT authors and activists were collected in the book We're Here, We're Queer. He edited the Mark Abramson memoir For My Brothers and co-edited Nothing Personal: Chronicles of Chicago's LGBTQ Community 1977–1997. He was also a contributor to Gay Press, Gay Power and wrote ten biographical essays for the LGBT history book Out and Proud in Chicago. He was the author of the Starz books (Starz, More Starz, Rising Starz, Ultimate Starz), a four-volume series of interviews with gay porn stars. He has had two queer monologues adapted for the stage, served as co-editor of the Windy City Times Pride Literary Supplement for several years, and was co-founder and former contributor to the horror film website RacksAndRazors.com. He lives in Chicago with his partner, Carl, and his two dogs, Flannery and Fitzgerald. He was inducted into the Chicago Gay and Lesbian Hall of Fame in 2011 and currently serves on the board of the organization.